THE RUNAWAY VISCOUNT

MATCHMAKING CHRONICLES
BOOK THREE

DARCY BURKE

Zealous Quill Press

The Runaway Viscount
Copyright © 2022 Darcy Burke
All rights reserved.
ISBN: 9781637261026

This is a work of fiction. Names, characters, places, and incidents
are the product of the author's imagination or are used
fictitiously. Any resemblance to actual events, locales, or persons,
living or dead, is purely coincidental.

Book design: © Darcy Burke.
Book Cover Design: © Dar Albert, Wicked Smart Designs.
Editing: Lindsey Faber.

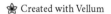 Created with Vellum

THE RUNAWAY VISCOUNT

Two years ago, independent widow Juliana Sheldon spent a blissful night with the Viscount Audlington at an inn during a snowstorm, and the next morning, he left without a word. Juliana doesn't realize how much his abandonment upset her until she encounters him at a matchmaking house party. He'd like to rekindle their affair, but Juliana prefers to torment him instead. Until she finally surrenders to temptation—only to be dismayed when he begins to talk about the one thing she doesn't want: marriage.

Lucas Trask, heir to an earldom, has left his rakish reputation behind in favor of finally taking a wife. He never forgot Juliana and reconnecting with her seems like fate is telling him who he should wed. However, Lucas has a secret, one he's never dared share with anyone. If he can convince Juliana to be his wife, he'll reveal everything. But when tragedy strikes, he must leave again. This time, the runaway viscount may be all out of luck.

Don't miss the rest of the *Matchmaking Chronicles*!

Do you want to hear all the latest about me and my books? Sign up at <u>Reader Club newsletter</u> for members-only bonus content, advance notice of pre-orders, insider scoop, as well as contests and giveaways!

Care to share your love for my books with like-minded readers? Want to hang with me and see pictures of my cats (who doesn't!)? Then don't miss my exclusive Facebook groups!

Darcy's Duchesses for historical readers
Burke's Book Lovers for contemporary readers

Want more historical romance? Do you like your historical romance filled with passion and red hot chemistry? Join me and my author friends in the Facebook group, Historical Harlots, for exclusive giveaways, chat with amazing HistRom authors, and more!

CHAPTER 1

Steeton, Yorkshire, January 1802

*T*he innkeeper's wife ushered Juliana Sheldon into the Pack Horse. "Come in and get warm, dear. You arrived just in time. I've one last room." She smiled brightly, her cheeks rosy and her blue eyes sparkling with cheer.

Juliana exhaled in relief. This was the third inn she'd tried in the past hour as the snow had coated the ground in ever-increasing thickness. Turning her head, she nodded toward her coachman, who hurried to take the coach and horses to the stable.

"Thank you so much," Juliana said as she pushed the hood of her cloak back, scattering wet droplets from the snow that had gathered on the wool. There were several tables in the common room with guests filling many of the chairs. A crackling fire burned within the large hearth at the back of the room.

"I'm pleased you found us. I'm Mrs. Lilley. It's chaotic at the moment, as I'm helping to prepare dinner." She brushed her hand against her apron and slid an errant brown strand of hair beneath her mobcap. "Your room is upstairs on the right at the end of the corridor. You're welcome to go up and remove your cloak and warm yourself. Dinner will be ready shortly."

"I'll do that, thank you, Mrs. Lilley." Juliana went to the stairs in the corner and climbed to the first floor, weary after her long day of travel in the snowstorm. She should have arrived home in Skipton by now, but the turnpike had become impassable. She was glad they'd found lodging at last.

She ought to have listened to her mother, who'd suggested she stay another day or two since it looked as if it might snow. However, after more than a fortnight visiting her parents, Juliana was eager to return to her small cottage at Foxland, the estate where she'd lived with her husband. When he'd died three years ago, his younger brother had inherited the estate, but her husband's will had provided her with a settlement and a place for her to call home.

Though the corridor was dim, Juliana found the door to her chamber and pushed inside. To her delight, a fire crackled in the hearth. The fireplace, like the rest of the room, was small, but more than adequate. Warming herself, she took in the bed and the small table with two spindly chairs. A worn, squashy, cushioned bench sat near the fire. Juliana went to hang her damp cloak on a hook near the door, then divested herself of her gloves and bonnet. She then scooted the bench closer to the hearth so she could sit and restore herself before going down for dinner.

"Is someone there?"

A masculine voice from the doorway drew Juliana to turn her head. A tall, athletic gentleman stood at the threshold. The door was half-open.

"Did I leave the door like that?" she asked, thinking she'd closed it and not at all certain what to make of this stranger barging in. Granted, he was a very well-dressed and tidy stranger, but he was still imposing on her space.

"Not quite *this* open, but it wasn't closed," he said. "I just thought I'd be friendly."

"It seems you're being intrusive. Shall I inform my husband of your presumption?"

"Er, no. I didn't mean to intrude. As I said, I was being friendly. Where is your husband? I should like to apologize."

She narrowed her eyes at him. "You should apologize to *me*."

"You're correct. My deepest apologies."

Juliana wondered if she was being uncharitable. She was exhausted and hungry, and just starting to feel warmth in her extremities. "It's all right. I'm irritable after the long day of travel, and this is the third inn I tried before finding a room."

"That's awful. I'm sorry to hear of your troubles." He smiled, his gaze darting about the room. "I'll leave you to it, then." He started to turn and to pull the door shut.

"Wait. I don't have a husband. I didn't mean to snap at you." Heat flushed her neck. "I'm not usually like that."

"It's understandable when you're tired and cold. And hungry perhaps?"

"Famished."

"If you're alone, I should be delighted to escort you downstairs."

Juliana stood and brushed her hands down her skirts. Her thick petticoat settled about her calves. Yes, she was much warmer and felt better overall. "Thank you."

She went to the door and saw he was quite

handsome. His elegantly sculpted features possessed a mischievous charm. Perhaps that was due to the slight smile that teased his full lips. His brows were thick and medium brown, a shade darker than his hair. Beneath them, his gray eyes sparked with interest as he regarded her. Did he realize she was studying him?

He pushed the door open more and held it while she stepped into the corridor.

Glancing back at him, she said, "Make sure you close it since I apparently did a poor job."

Pulling it closed, he frowned slightly. "It doesn't latch easily. I don't think it was your fault. And I *am* sorry for invading your space."

Juliana hated that she'd said anything. She had a bad habit of speaking without always considering how it might come out, especially when it involved her space. She valued her privacy and independence, two things her brother-in-law couldn't seem to respect. He visited her cottage without notice, sometimes coming inside after only a brief knock, and it greatly pricked her ire.

"There, now it's closed properly," he said. "Shall we go down?"

"Thank you. I'm Mrs. Sheldon."

"I thought you said you didn't have a husband."

"He died three years ago." She cocked her head. "Did you think I'd travel alone as an unwed young lady?" Not that she was young—she was twenty-nine.

"Good point. I'm afraid I was far too fixed on your marital state to consider propriety." He laughed. "Bad habit when I meet an attractive woman."

Her pulse picked up speed at his compliment. "Are you a rake, then?" She'd heard about men like him and suspected she'd met one or two, but her experience was limited.

He laughed again. "Some would say so, though I prefer not to characterize myself in that manner."

"Yet you meet a woman and immediately try to determine whether—" She stopped as she discovered she wasn't sure what he was doing. "Are you hoping I am wed or not?" Perhaps he preferred to pursue a woman he wouldn't be forced to wed. That matched what she knew about rakish behavior.

He grimaced faintly. "Now you've backed me into a corner. Unwed young ladies are trouble since I am not yet in the market for a wife."

"So you would prefer I were wed." She frowned. "Or widowed."

"As I said, you've neatly cornered me. Now I can't deny rakish tendencies when I admit that I enjoy meeting attractive widows, particularly so far from London where one can find a modicum of discretion."

Juliana couldn't help smiling. "At least you're honest about it. Now I know what you're about and why you were poking yourself into my chamber."

He held up his hand, a look of distress flitting across his features. "That was *not* my intent, I assure you. I really was just trying to be friendly." He ran his hands through his hair, tousling it in a thoroughly rakish way. Or what she imagined a rake might do.

"I see," she murmured, amused by his discomfort.

"Let me start again." He presented an elegant leg and bowed extravagantly. "Allow me to introduce myself. I am Lucas Trask, the Viscount Audlington."

A viscount! She'd met an earl and a baron. The Earl of Cosford was a friend of her husband's, and he was actually heir to a dukedom. He and Vincent had gone to school together. Juliana had visited Blickton, Cosford's estate, on a handful of occasions during her marriage. Lady Cosford was delightful and had invited Juliana to visit a few times since Vincent's death, but the timing hadn't been convenient.

And the baron lived near Skipton. He was ninety and in possession of a foul sense of humor. Juliana liked him immensely.

She curtsied. "I'm pleased to make your acquaintance. I'm Mrs. Juliana Sheldon."

"Lovely." He offered his arm. "May I escort you to dinner?"

"Certainly." She put her hand on his sleeve, and he guided her down the stairs. "Where are you on your way to?"

"Northwich—my family seat southwest of Manchester. You?"

"I'm on my way home to Skipton after visiting my parents in Leeds for Yuletide."

He glanced in her direction as they reached the common room. "You're eager to be home?"

She took her hand from his arm and turned to look at him. "How did you know?"

"Epiphany was just yesterday, and I might have thought the weather would have prevented you from leaving today. But it did not." He lifted a shoulder. "Consequently, I gathered you wanted to return home."

"Excellent deduction. Yes, I like my house and my horse."

"And your parents...less so?"

"I adore them actually, but nearly three weeks with them is plenty."

He grinned. "I feel the same about my parents. They are wonderful people, but as I am now thirty-one and unwed, there is a nearly constant expectation from them. It can grow tiresome, even though I know they mean well."

Juliana nodded in agreement. "I can relate to that quite fervently. My mother especially hopes I will wed again despite my telling her that I am quite happy at present. But you are right—they do mean well."

He sent her an understanding glance. "This year, I spent Yuletide with other relatives and am now going to see my parents before I continue on to London for the Season."

Of course, he would spend the Season in London. He was a viscount and a rake. If he was a viscount and still had a father, that meant he was in line for an even greater title, probably an earldom. Juliana lived comfortably and couldn't imagine such a sophisticated life.

"Are there great demands on you in London?" she asked.

"Ah, I wouldn't say they are *great*." He looked about the common room, which was quite full and hummed with noise. "The inn is full, it seems."

"Yes, I was given the last room. I suppose we should find a table." She started to turn, then stopped, facing him once more. "I shouldn't assume you wanted to sit together."

"I would enjoy that. Otherwise, we'll both be dining alone, isn't that right? Actually, I daresay the inn is crowded enough to necessitate our dining together. As it happens, I'd very much like to continue our conversation."

Would he? She suppressed a smile. After three years alone—well, not completely alone, she had a lovely circle of friends in Skipton—she had to admit it was rather nice to speak with a gentleman. An attractive viscount, no less.

"Shall we sit over here?" She indicated an empty table somewhat near the fire.

"Splendid."

As she turned, his hand grazed her lower back. It was the barest touch, but her breath stalled as tingles of awareness raced through her. She hadn't been touched by a man in well more than three years.

He held her chair as she sat, and she was no longer annoyed by the exhausting day or the fact that her travel had been delayed. She could think of far worse things than being stranded at an inn with a charming viscount.

A serving maid brought a tray and asked if they preferred wine or ale. They both chose wine. "Dinner will be served shortly." She bustled off, clearly busy with so many people there.

Juliana clasped her hands in her lap. "What is it you do in London, my lord?"

"The typical things one does in a Season."

"And what things are those?"

"You didn't have one?" He held up his hand. "That's awfully presumptuous of me. My apologies. Not everyone has a Season."

She appreciated his belated self-awareness. "Count me among those who did not. I grew up in Leeds. My father is a bookseller."

"Again, I'm sorry. It's just that you look as though you could have taken London by storm." His eyes glinted with respect. "You're certainly self-possessed enough to have been a great success."

Juliana laughed softly. "You've only just met me."

"You had no compunction about calling out my intrusive behavior. You don't simper, and I am willing to wager you never have. Since your father is a bookseller, I assume you are well-read and highly intelligent."

She couldn't help but feel flattered that he saw her in such a way. "You're more observant than most people."

"I try to be. I find people interesting. *That's* what I do in London—I watch people, and hopefully, I learn."

"What do you learn?"

"Whom to avoid, mostly." He smirked as he shook his head. "Some of London Society can be quite brutal."

"In what way?"

"Mostly, they are self-serving. Trying to find ways to climb to greater heights. To deepen their pockets or improve their standing."

"I can imagine you are a target for women seeking a brilliant match for their daughters. I assume your father is an earl or similar?"

"The Earl of Northwich. And yes, I've spent the last decade fending off marriage-minded mothers and their daughters."

"A decade? That has to have taken a great deal of skill." She cocked her head to the side. "But I thought you were a rake. Surely they wouldn't want their daughters to wed someone with such a reputation."

"With a title on offer, you'd be surprised," he said sardonically. "Furthermore, as far as rakes go, there are others who are far worse—I don't spend my nights in brothels or gaming hells." He rushed to say, "Pardon me for mentioning such things in your presence. You've made me far too comfortable, Mrs. Sheldon."

"Please don't stop. I've only been to London

once—for a week after I married Vincent. I was young and eager to visit Paternoster Row."

"The bookselling street. Of course you were. Is that where you spent your time?"

"Not much of it, unfortunately. Vincent was more inclined to visit the museums, which I enjoyed."

"What of evening entertainment? Did you visit the theater or a pleasure garden, perhaps?"

"No, Vincent didn't want to spend the extra money. I was hoping we might go to Vauxhall." She shrugged. "Still, it was a nice trip."

"Much has changed in the last decade. You should visit again. If you come during the Season, send me word and I'll squire you about town."

"Wouldn't that provoke gossip? The unknown widow from Yorkshire on the arm of the rakish viscount?"

"Well, now I'll be disappointed if you don't come." He pressed his lips into a mock pout that drew her attention to his mouth. "I'll make sure they call you mysterious."

Juliana laughed. "Do you have so much power?"

"Probably not, but I do know an astounding number of people, and I *think* the vast majority of them like me. If I tell them you're mysterious, they'll likely repeat that."

"All right, then. I'm the Mysterious Widow and you're the Rakish Viscount. Sounds as though someone should write novels about us."

"You're the book expert. Have you thought about writing one?"

"Oh no, I couldn't. I wouldn't even know where to begin."

"How about with 'Once upon a time…'"

The serving maid returned with their wine, depositing the glasses on the table without a word.

"How original of you," Juliana said. She picked up her glass and took a sip. "I might try something more exciting, such as 'Long ago, in the days before stories were written down...'"

His gaze locked with hers. "Well, now I'm utterly captivated. I think you must pen a tale."

A blast of cold air filled the common room as the door opened. "Go on in," the woman said to three children while holding a fourth. They moved inside, and the woman closed the door.

Mrs. Lilley met them, wiping her hands on her apron. Juliana and the viscount were close enough to hear what was said.

"I'm so sorry, but I don't have any rooms," Mrs. Lilley said, her brow creasing as her gaze fell on the children.

The poor woman, her face red from the cold, looked completely defeated. "I think we've been to every inn. My husband took our cart to the stable. The groom outside said there was room for it and our horses."

"Yes, we do have more space in the stables." Mrs. Lilley grimaced as she glanced toward the stairs. "The best I can offer is dinner and a space by the fire tonight. And some blankets."

Lord Audlington suddenly stood. He went to Mrs. Lilley. "My room could certainly support this family. There's a large bed and ample space to make more beds on the floor."

Mrs. Lilley's eyes rounded. "But where will you sleep, my lord?"

"I can make do down here. I insist."

The mother sniffed. "Thank you, my lord."

"It's the least I can do." He went to the table closest to the fire where a couple was sitting and gave them a smile that Juliana was sure charmed everyone he encountered. "I'm sure you don't mind moving so this family can warm up after their travails."

"Not at all," the man responded. They relocated to another table.

Audlington ushered the cold woman and children to the fireside table. "Dinner will be here very soon. Then we'll get you up to your chamber."

The serving maid set down platters of food, startling Juliana. She'd been so focused on the viscount that she'd completely missed the young woman's approach. The fragrant scent of stew filled Juliana's nostrils, and her stomach rumbled. "Thank you."

Looking back to the viscount, she saw that he'd returned to Mrs. Lilley. Now he made his way back to their table. "Ah, dinner," he said pleasantly and nonchalantly, as if he hadn't just behaved in a thoroughly heroic manner. "It smells divine."

"That was incredibly kind of you," Juliana said.

He'd picked up a thick slice of bread and was now slathering it with butter. "Anyone would have done it."

"No one else did, though. Not even me." She looked down at her food. "Perhaps we should give them our food."

"I believe they are busy warming themselves at the moment," he said after glancing toward their table. "And I'm confident their dinner will arrive with due haste. Do not fret over not offering your room. To be fair, it's rather small. They'll be more comfortable in my chamber. There's a large four-poster bed that will likely fit the mother and two of the children plus the father. Then there is also a small bed for a maid or valet. A pair of the children can easily share that. It's unlikely they even need to make additional beds on the floor now that I think about it." He took a bite of bread.

"You are completely unaware of how wonderfully you've behaved." It wasn't just giving them his room; it was also making sure they'd be warm by the fire. She recalled that he'd gone back to speak with Mrs. Lilley. "You're paying for their lodging, aren't you?"

He only shrugged as he spooned his stew. He was not at all what she expected from a rakish viscount.

"Where will you sleep?" she asked.

"Mrs. Lilley will give me some blankets, and I'll make a bed on the floor here."

"Do you really think you'll be able to sleep down here?" It was a rhetorical question. "Sleep on the floor in my chamber instead. It's small, but at least you can have a modicum of privacy."

"Not from you." He waggled his brows, and she couldn't help but smile.

"If we turn our backs to each other while we prepare for bed, it will be fine."

He picked up his spoon. "I'm not sure what you mean by 'fine,' but I assure you that if we inhabit the same space, everything about it will be more than fine. And whether you turn your back to me while you disrobe or not, I will still be exceedingly aware of your presence and the fact that I find you more than passingly attractive." His gaze had been fixed on her while he spoke, and now the gray seemed to glitter like silver. "*Much* more."

Juliana shifted in her chair as a heat she hadn't felt in a long time pervaded every part of her. It seemed she was going to spend at least the next two nights—there was no way the roads would be passable by tomorrow, even if it stopped snowing right this moment—with a flirtatious, rakish, and thoroughly arousing viscount.

"That means you'll accept my invitation?" Her voice rasped, as if she'd inhaled cobwebs.

His lips curled into a beguiling smile. "How can I resist your kind hospitality?"

Another flash of heat passed through her. This could become dangerous. She lifted her wineglass and brought it to her lips, speaking over the rim. "What a diverting trip this has turned out to be."

"I will certainly hope so." His voice crackled with anticipation.

What scandalous mischief had Juliana got herself into?

~

*L*ucas watched the firelight cast dancing shadows across the ceiling. His makeshift bed of blankets and a few pillows on the floor was not particularly comfortable, but he was warm near the fire at least. Turning his head, he looked toward the bed, the head of which was against the opposite wall, and wondered if Mrs. Sheldon could say the same. Hopefully, she was comfortable *and* warm.

They'd flirted all through dinner and then played backgammon until her exhaustion got the better of her. When she yawned more than she moved pieces, he insisted she retire. She'd seemed grateful and bid him good night.

He'd lingered for an hour after that, giving her plenty of time to complete her toilet and go to bed without him being a nuisance. Mrs. Lilley had offered to move a settee from their living quarters into the common room for him to sleep upon, but he'd declined. He'd yet to meet a settee that could support his long frame. She'd given him several blankets and pillows instead, which he'd brought upstairs to his new chamber, along with his things, which had been delivered from his former room, after Mrs. Lilley had gone to bed.

Once he'd fashioned the bed near the fire, he'd stripped down to his shirt and smallclothes before tucking himself inside. He had yet to find sleep.

He looked again toward the bed, wondering if Mrs. Sheldon had been more fortunate. He had to think so. She'd seemed beyond tired, and her breathing was deep and even, if that signified anything. He could barely make her out beneath the bedclothes. Was she warm enough?

Pushing the blanket away, he got to his feet and stoked the fire. Now he would be hot, but that was a small price if it meant she would be cozy. Satisfied that it was providing more heat, he moved his bed farther from the hearth.

This brought him closer to the bed. He couldn't resist taking a step toward it.

Mrs. Sheldon sat up, and he reared back, startled.

"Thank you." Her sable hair hung in a thick plait over her shoulder with the curls at the end caressing her breast. There was a vibrance to the dark, rich color that he found magnificent. He longed to run his fingers through the locks to determine their texture and to lean close to inhale their scent.

He jerked his gaze from her before he stared like a desperate swain. "For what?"

"The fire. I was cold."

"I thought you were sleeping."

"Not really. I haven't been able to get warm. I typically have a warming pan, but I didn't want to ask for one. Mrs. Lilley was terribly busy."

"Would you like one of my blankets?" He started toward his pallet.

"No, thank you, I couldn't. It's bad enough you're sleeping on the floor. I couldn't take one of your blankets."

He looked at her again, glad for the shadows that fell across her. "You've already been kind enough to invite me to sleep here instead of the common room."

"And I shan't ruin that by robbing you of what's left of your comfort."

"It's all right, truly. My bed is actually quite snug. I moved it away from the fire, in fact."

"Perhaps we should change places. You sleep here, and I'll take the pallet."

"Absolutely not." He shook his head. "That bed is likely a hundred times more comfortable than the pallet, even if it is farther from the hearth."

"But you said your bed was nice." She sounded like she was frowning.

"It's warm. It's more than adequate." He picked up the blanket that had covered him and took it to the bed. "Here, this is warm from the fire. I'll trade you this for one of yours. Will you agree to that at least?" He put the blanket over her to make his argument for him.

She let out a soft mewl of delight that stirred every part of his body into taut awareness. "This is lovely, thank you." She pulled a blanket from the bedclothes and tossed it toward him. He grabbed it as she worked the blanket he'd given her into the bed, presumably so it was directly next to her.

The one she'd given him was also warm. It also smelled of her—the faint scent of flowers and spice. He didn't doubt for a moment that he'd got the better end of the bargain.

"You should just sleep with me," she said.

He froze. "What did you say?"

"If we slept together, we'd both be warm. It was

the only thing I missed about sleeping with my husband—he snored dreadfully. Indeed, I moved to my own chamber a year into the marriage."

"I'm sorry to hear that. That he snored, I mean." Lucas didn't think he snored. None of his bed partners had ever complained anyway.

"That wasn't the most disappointing thing, actually. He'd also become less…interested in bed sport."

Oh hell. Did she have to mention that? His mind was already struggling not to imagine her in all manner of explicit, sensual activities, all of them beginning with when he slipped into that bed with her.

He was considering it, wasn't he?

Of course he was. He wasn't a fool. He was a warm-blooded man with a healthy appetite for sex. Plus, he found her irresistibly attractive in both body and mind. She was an engaging conversationalist—bright and witty—and he found himself eager to spend more time in her company, even if they only played backgammon. Perhaps that was because she didn't treat him as if he were a prize to be won. Most women tried to either entice him into their bed or woo him into marriage.

"That is, ah, disconcerting," was all he managed to say.

She threw the covers back. "Come on, then. We'll just be sleeping."

Had she contemplated more than that? He couldn't bring himself to ask. One answer would disappoint him, and the other would drive his arousal to new heights. As it was, his cock already stood at the ready. He glanced down and saw that his shirt hung oddly because of his erection. Surely she would notice that, if she hadn't already.

"I promise to keep my hands to myself." No matter how hard it would be.

"Well, if we're to provide warmth for one another, it would be better if we touched. But if you're referring to touching me in a way that would be inappropriate, I understand and appreciate that. Now, get in, because I'm getting cold again."

Against his better judgment, he slid into the bedclothes and pulled them up. She burrowed beneath the covers and moved toward him.

"Would it be inappropriate?" she asked, her legs brushing his. "If we touched, I mean. It's not as if you can ruin me. I'm an independent widow. If I wanted to have a tryst with you in this bed, who's to say it's not completely appropriate?" She almost sounded as though she were having a conversation with herself, as if she were making a case for seducing him.

He nearly laughed—there was no need for seduction. He would gladly tup her faster than she could say, "Touch me, please."

"You are the only one who can say whether it would be appropriate or not," he said evenly while his body raged with desire.

She pressed her side against his, positioned on her back as he was. "I suppose that's true. Except you would need to be a willing participant as well." She turned her head toward him. "I, for one, somewhat miss sleeping with another person, particularly at this time of year. It's cozy and comforting." She moved her leg against his again. "What is your opinion?"

Bloody hell, was she asking him if he wanted to shag her? Or did she just miss the companionship of sleeping with someone? Lucas couldn't really speak to that, as he could probably count the number of times he'd spent an entire night in bed with a woman on both hands. "Mrs. Sheldon, how long has it been since you shared a bed with a man?"

"Seven years. Since I took my own chamber in my husband's house. But I think you mean the act of sex. That's been about five, when Vincent and I stopped sharing a bed entirely. The mutual attraction we once shared, that had driven us to wed, had completely cooled. I wonder if that happens with all marriages, but then I look to my parents, and it seems that is not the case. They were a love match and continue to be."

"Mine are too," Lucas said, fascinated by this woman who so boldly discussed things most women didn't, whether they were widows or not. "Were you and your husband? A love match, I mean."

"No. We were a lust match, and when that dissipated, we settled into an easy friendship. I suppose that's better than estrangement. I was sad when he died."

That sounded perfectly horrid. Not just that he'd died, but that their marriage had started with promise and become something less than they'd expected. He realized he feared that. His parents had demonstrated what it was like for two people to be madly in love, and then his younger brother had gone and done the same when he'd wed last year after falling desperately for his wife.

Meanwhile, Lucas didn't even keep a mistress. He preferred short affairs or single trysts. It was much easier to get away without any fuss.

Mrs. Sheldon could be a brief liaison.

For some reason, he didn't want to group her with his other lovers. She was different somehow. Unexpected.

Because he'd encountered her in the middle of a snowstorm and now found himself sharing a bed with her for nonsexual purposes. He chuckled.

"What do you find amusing?" she asked, sounding bemused.

"I like you, Mrs. Sheldon. But I must insist you sleep. You practically collapsed on the backgammon board earlier."

She yawned. "You had to go and remind me. All right. Let's sleep. I am much warmer now, thank you. I hope this isn't a terrible imposition." She wriggled against him, and he swallowed a moan.

"It is a distinct pleasure," he murmured, thinking she might already be asleep as her breathing had evened once more. For the first time, he perhaps understood the appeal of sharing a bed with someone every night. "Good night, Mrs. Sheldon."

CHAPTER 2

*L*ucas awakened early, just as daylight peeked through the curtains and speckled across the floor. He blinked, a moment passing before he realized where he was. And with whom.

Mrs. Sheldon's—hell, he may as well think of her as Juliana after sharing a bed with her—leg was entwined with his, her back pressed against his side. The plait of her hair lay across his shoulder. He now knew it smelled of lavender. But he still couldn't say how it felt. He practically itched to loosen the strands.

Most mornings, he awoke with a stiff cock, but today was worse. Today fairly begged for his hand to ease his suffering. He would not submit to self-pleasure while he occupied the same room as Juliana. No matter how badly he was tempted.

Instead, he reluctantly slipped from the warm bed and quickly dressed. He stoked the fire, taking care to be quieter than last night, which meant it took longer. Satisfied that Juliana would be warm enough, he took his leave, ensuring the door was latched closed behind him.

After relieving himself in the privy, he considered meeting his other needs, but it was too bloody cold. It had stopped snowing at least, and the sun would likely turn the snow to slush by midday. Still, he couldn't travel today. He would hope for tomorrow.

Would he really? He had to admit he was enjoying spending time with Juliana. And sharing her bed, even if they were just sleeping. He felt particularly rested this morning.

Back inside, Mrs. Lilley greeted him. "Would you care for coffee or tea to warm you, my lord?"

"Tea, thank you." He'd never developed a taste for coffee. He'd drink it on occasion, but would always choose tea if he had the option.

He sat at the same table he'd shared with Juliana last night. His father would tell him he was being typically nostalgic, like his mother. It was true. Lucas possessed a sentimental nature that his father did not. Sometimes he wondered how his parents were a love match in spite of how different they could be.

Mrs. Lilley brought his tea and poured out for him, adding sugar. "I trust you passed a pleasant night?"

"I did, thank you."

"I noticed you did not sleep in the common room." She didn't ask a question, but her curiosity was as loud as a thunderstorm.

He would not appease it, however. "I did not." Picking up his tea, he sipped the delicious brew.

With a shrug, Mrs. Lilley informed him that she'd bring breakfast shortly. Then she left the common room.

A few minutes later, Juliana appeared on the staircase. The plait of her dark hair was wound and pinned atop her head, exposing the sleek column of her neck. She wore the same gown as yesterday, a pretty but simple traveling piece of peacock blue wool. "You're up very early," she said, coming to join him at the table.

"Did you sleep well?" he asked, wishing he'd thought to request a second cup so he could offer her tea.

"Oh yes, thanks to you." She smiled widely, and he was suddenly breathless. He felt as if he were a lad at Oxford again, nervously approaching a woman for the first time. "It stopped snowing."

"It did, though the roads won't start thawing until later. Tomorrow will be the earliest we can depart, and that's only if it doesn't snow again."

She glanced toward the window that looked out into the yard. "The sky looked fairly clear to me. Perhaps we will be lucky."

"You're still anxious to get home," he said.

"Perhaps a little less so." A small smile teased her dark pink lips. The lower one was fuller than the upper, perfect for him to tug on with his teeth. Her face was the shape of a heart with a slight dimple in her chin. But it was her piercing green eyes that most often drew his attention. They were sharp with intelligence, as well as captivating in a mysterious way, as if she possessed secrets. But didn't they all?

Feet clambered down the stairs as the mother who'd arrived last night led her three children, while she again carried the fourth, to the common room. Her husband followed at the rear. He'd come into the common room to join his family for dinner, then he'd thanked Lucas for giving them his room. He'd also tried to reimburse him for the cost, but Lucas had told him to save it in the event they ran into further challenges on their journey.

"Can we play in the snow, Mama?" one of the two boys asked.

"You'll get wet, and then we'll have to dry your

clothes. No, we'll be staying inside today. Now get to the table so we can eat our breakfast." She ushered them to the table by the fire once more.

The children slid onto their chairs looking rather downcast.

"I remember what it feels like not to be allowed to do something." He glanced toward Juliana. "Do you?"

"All the time. I'm a woman, remember?" She laughed softly. "It's slightly better now that I am widowed. There were many times when I was young and unmarried when I would want to go somewhere or do something, and my mother said I could not."

"What sorts of things?"

Mrs. Lilley returned with a second cup for Juliana and poured more steaming water into the pot. "I've bread, ham, and eggs coming out shortly."

Juliana smiled up at her. "Thank you, Mrs. Lilley."

"I'm glad to see you've formed an association," she said, looking from Juliana to Lucas. "Mayhap I'll get to brag to my friends that a viscount discovered his bride at *my* inn." Her gaze held a knowing glimmer, as if she'd deduced where Lucas had spent the night. To her credit, she didn't verbalize that.

"I'm sorry to disappoint you, Mrs. Lilley, but his lordship and I are not betrothed, nor will we be," Juliana said.

"Ah well, I can hope." Mrs. Lilley took herself off, and Juliana poured her tea.

"How do you know we won't become betrothed? Now that you've said that, we'll likely wed and have ten children."

Juliana laughed. "I don't think so. Definitely not

the children, anyway." She sipped her tea. "Mrs. Lilley was only teasing."

Probably, but Lucas was suddenly thinking of whether Juliana could be his viscountess. A chill ran down his neck, which was what typically happened when he considered marriage. He never failed to feel constrained, as if he were suddenly confined to a small, windowless room. It was terribly silly, and he couldn't understand why, especially when the sensation passed as quickly as it appeared.

He sought to change the subject and looked toward the moping children once more. "You didn't tell me what you wanted to do that your mother wouldn't allow."

"There was one time when I wanted to ride in a boat on the river with some friends. That was forbidden. As was playing badminton in the park. Unless my mother was there. But that wasn't as fun." Her magnificent eyes glittered with that enigmatic coyness he found so alluring.

"Surely you stole away and did those things."

"A few times. Until I was caught and sentenced to my room for a fortnight. I followed the rules after that."

"You regret doing so?"

"Not really. I had a very happy childhood, and my parents are incredibly kindhearted. They only wanted what was best for me."

"And that was marriage to Sheldon?"

"They were delighted when he asked for my hand. He owned a large estate with an excellent income. Papa had thought I might marry a clerk or, if I were lucky, a barrister."

"How did you and Sheldon meet?" Lucas wanted to hear every part of her story.

"He came into my father's shop one day looking

for some treatise about sheep or other. I can't remember exactly. We, ah, formed a connection immediately."

"Not love, because you said you weren't in love with each other." Actually, he recalled she'd only said she hadn't loved him. "Unless…did he fall in love with you?"

She shook her head. "It was far more base. Instant lust if you will."

"Well, I've certainly experienced that." With her, in fact. Perhaps not *instantly*, but within a short amount of time upon making her acquaintance. He supposed sharing a bed with someone to whom you were attracted would do that.

Little pleats furrowed into her brow. "Yet you haven't married anyone about whom you felt that way?"

"No, I would want to feel something more than that, I think." When she looked away, he realized she was thinking of her marriage. "It's not a bad reason to wed someone," he said quietly.

"Thank you for saying that." She exhaled. "I was young and probably foolish. And I did think it was more at the time."

"You don't seem unhappy."

"I'm not. Unlike those children." She sent a look in their direction. One of the boys was talking to his father, and it seemed he was perhaps pleading his case to be allowed outside.

"My brother and I would be throwing snowballs at each other in the yard." Lucas smiled, recalling the many times they'd pummeled each other until they were soaked. "I'm eager to get home to see him, actually. If it snows, perhaps we'll have a snowball fight like we did in our youth."

"Your family sounds lovely."

"It's about to expand. The reason I'm hurrying

home is because his wife is due to deliver their first child very soon."

"How wonderful. I have two nieces and three nephews. They are delightful. Exhausting, but delightful."

Lucas realized he'd never asked if she had children. He assumed she did not since they weren't traveling with her. Surely they would have visited her parents too. "You and Sheldon didn't have children."

She shook her head. "I have to think I can't be a mother. We certainly exerted enough effort for at least one or two." She blushed. "There I go again, sharing too much."

He leaned over the table and whispered, "I like knowing everything about you."

Her eyes met his. "Oh."

Mrs. Lilley delivered their breakfasts and apologized for the delay. They ate for a few minutes in silence. Lucas couldn't tell if not having children bothered her, but didn't want to ask. While he was curious, he didn't want to be intrusive.

"Will you be looking for a viscountess this Season?" she asked before taking a bite of ham.

"Vaguely. That's what I typically do. I find the Marriage Mart fatiguing. It's such a performance, and it's difficult to get to know a person with all the bloody rules preventing you from doing so. I could never have had this much time or fascinating conversation with a young unmarried lady."

"Not to mention the sleeping together," she said slyly.

He laughed. "Not to mention *that*. Highly frowned upon."

"Then the Marriage Mart was definitely *not* for me." Her tone was a bit haughty, in a playful way, and he couldn't keep from smiling. Why couldn't he have met someone like her during a London Season?

She picked up her tea. "What do you do besides avoid the parson's trap? Are you in Parliament?"

"I am not. I amuse myself and continue to help my father oversee our family interests."

"If you aren't a member of Parliament and you don't wish to attend the Marriage Mart, why attend the Season at all?"

"What a disturbingly trenchant question." He nodded at her in admiration. "You've cut straight to the heart of my meaningless existence. I am a rake without purpose. Well, good purpose anyway." He was joking, but he couldn't ignore the needle of discomfort jabbing the back of his mind.

"Why not find something else to occupy you, then? Or, and this is a truly scandalous idea, *don't go to London*." She gasped and arched her brows before smiling mischievously.

She'd given him something to think about. Many things, actually. He never had trouble occupying himself outside London. He had many friends and enjoyed traveling to visit their houses. Often, he spent time touring their estates and gathering ideas on improvements. He enjoyed speaking with the tenants and learning about their lives. Indeed, weren't those visits far more engaging than the Season? Furthermore, wasn't it possible—and preferable—that he could find a wife on such an occasion? His friend Cosford and his lovely wife typically hosted entertaining house parties. Perhaps they wouldn't mind assembling one for the purpose of matchmaking.

"Thank you, Papa!"

Lucas turned his head toward the child who'd exclaimed in joy.

"Only ten minutes. And no snowballs. You can't get soaking wet!"

"Forgive me," Lucas said, rising. "I'm afraid my services are required." He strode toward the family. "If you're amenable, I'd like to offer myself up as target. The children may throw all the snowballs they wish—at me. Of course, they have to actually hit me, and I can move very quickly."

The three children, who'd all left their chairs, gazed up at him with excitement.

"Can we, Papa?" the eldest boy asked, sending a pleading look toward his father.

"Upstairs to get your coats," the man said, taking the youngest from his wife, who guided the children upstairs to bundle up.

"I'll keep them as dry as possible," Lucas vowed.

"I thank you, my lord." He shook his head. "I'd never thought to meet a viscount, and I certainly never expected him to be as kind and...ordinary as you." He grimaced slightly. "My apologies. I didn't mean to say you were ordinary."

"I will take that as a great compliment." He returned to the table and finished his bread.

Juliana looked up at him, her eyes dazzlingly brilliant. "You continue to astonish me."

That hadn't been his intent, but he couldn't deny he enjoyed the thrill it gave him to hear it. "You're welcome to join us."

"Only if I get to throw snowballs at you too."

He leaned down and spoke close to her ear. "You may do whatever you like to me."

&

*A*fter dinner concluded, Juliana finished her toilet and perched on the bed. She couldn't remember spending a more wonderful day. She and the children had pelted Lucas with snowballs until he was rather soaked, prompting Mrs. Lilley to insist he take a warm bath in a private chamber off the kitchen. Juliana had tried not to think of Lucas nude in the bath.

Lucas.

He'd demanded she call him that, saying she owed him that much after likely causing him to catch a nasty cold. She'd felt horrible then, even realizing that he'd been teasing.

Now, as she sat on the edge of the bed awaiting his arrival, she prayed he didn't actually become ill. Though, there'd been no sign of that. He'd been charming and flirtatious as usual, in addition to amusing the children since they'd begged to be allowed to dine with Lucas.

Mrs. Lilley had pushed two tables together so Juliana and Lucas could share dinner with the Garretts. Mrs. Garret had sat beside Juliana, which had allowed Juliana the opportunity to hold their youngest, a sweet girl called Maggie who had recently celebrated her second birthday.

Then Mrs. Garrett had said that Juliana would make an excellent mother and of course his lordship had already demonstrated his skill at fatherhood. Juliana hadn't bothered to tell the woman that they weren't betrothed.

The door opened, drawing Juliana's attention. Lucas stopped short.

"I thought you'd be snuggled beneath the bedclothes by now." He closed the door securely.

"I was waiting for you. And thinking about dinner. I am fairly certain Mrs. Garrett assumed we are betrothed."

Lucas chuckled. "I wondered the same thing. She made a comment about how we would make excellent parents."

"You will, I'm sure," Juliana said. "If that interests you. You seem to love children." She recalled his anticipation at greeting his new niece or nephew.

"I do, actually, but I haven't considered what sort of father I'd be. Or when I'd become one. Seems premature when I've yet to meet a woman I want to wed."

Juliana didn't say so, but she hoped he would find someone and that he would have children. She could see he wanted them, even if he couldn't, and Mrs. Garrett was right that he'd make an excellent father.

Lucas removed his coat and hung it on a hook before facing her, one brow arched. "This is incredibly domestic." He sat in one of the chairs and removed his boots. He paused in taking off his stockings.

Juliana slid off the bed and went to him. "It would be even more so if I undressed you, don't you think?"

"Dear God, Juliana, your flirtation grows ever bolder. I might wonder if you are trying to seduce me." He tossed his second stocking to the floor and wiggled his toes.

She laughed softly. "Would it take much effort?"

He sat straight in the chair and began to unbutton his waistcoat. This casual removal of his clothing while she watched was incredibly and shockingly erotic. "Are we still flirting, or are we speaking frankly?"

Her body tensed with both anticipation and apprehension. "Since we are almost certainly leaving tomorrow and it's likely we'll never see each other again, I think we ought to be perfectly forthright, don't you?"

"You make an excellent argument." He shrugged

out of the waistcoat, and she took it from him, folding it in half and smoothing her hand over the rich fabric before laying it over the back of the other chair. "Very domestic," he murmured, his eyes slitting as he perused her.

She wore a thick dressing gown over her night rail, but his hot gaze made her feel as if she wasn't wearing a stitch. "I think we should go to bed," she said huskily. "And not to sleep."

A flicker of surprise danced over his features, but was quickly replaced with stark desire. "I am not opposed to that."

She moved to stand between his legs and plucked his cravat loose. "I shouldn't think so. Unless you've been bamming me this entire time. I was willing to wager you were *eager*."

He put his hands on her waist, and her knees threatened to buckle. It was the most intimate way he'd touched her, including when they'd slept together. "I am not eager," he said softly. "I am *desperate*. Please deliver me from my torment."

Juliana smiled. "We can't have you suffering." She pulled the cravat from him and let it fall to the floor. Sliding her hands into his shirt, she pressed her palms against his warm flesh. Then she lowered her head and put her lips against his.

His fingers dug into her through her garments as he kissed her with a bright intensity. He teased and played with his lips and tongue before moving one of his hands to her nape. Clasping her tightly, he deepened the kiss, showing her just how desperate he was.

Sensation spiraled through her, shocking her after so much time. She clutched his shoulders as it seemed the floor might melt beneath her feet.

He let go of her neck and unfastened her dressing gown, pushing it open and ending their kiss. "You're wearing a night rail," he said with grave disappointment.

"Poor planning on my part." She pulled her arms from the dressing gown and let it pool to the floor. Then she began to do the same with the night rail.

Lucas offered his assistance, pushing up the hem to expose her thighs, her sex, her abdomen. Before she removed the garment completely, his hands were on her breasts as he murmured unintelligible things. Juliana cast her head back and gave herself over to his touch. He caressed and tweaked, stoking a keen arousal that pulsed in her sex.

His mouth closed over one nipple. Moaning, she looked down at his head nestled against her and thrust her hands into his tawny hair. He drew on her flesh with his lips as his fingers squeezed her other nipple, tugging so that she arched toward him for more.

She whispered his name. "Now *I'm* desperate."

"Good." He skimmed his hand down over her abdomen to her hip, then inward to her sex. He teased her folds, his fingers moving against her. "You even *feel* desperate. How marvelous."

He suddenly stood and she half expected him to pick her up and toss her onto the bed. Instead, he reached for her hair and began to pluck the pins from it. "I have longed to see your hair down since nearly the moment I saw you."

The plait fell down her back, and she brought it forward over her shoulder. Before she could loosen it, he took over, untying the small ribbon at the end, then sliding his fingers through the locks and pulling them free.

Arranging her hair about her shoulders, Lucas

gazed at her with a near reverence. "So beautiful," he whispered before sweeping her into his arms.

He bore her to the bed, where he laid her carefully in the bedclothes. She watched as he removed the rest of his clothing. His body gleamed in the firelight, giving his flesh a golden cast. He was muscular, with a patch of tawny curls between his nipples that trailed down his belly. Following that path, she met the clear sign of *his* desperation. His cock stood tall and hard, as ready as she was.

"Come to me, Lucas. Now. We can go slower later."

He moved onto the bed, covering her body with his. "Later?"

"You can't think I'm going to squander a moment of this night."

He kissed her hard and fast, laughing. "You are an amazing woman. This is simply the best travel inconvenience I've ever experienced."

Juliana reached between them to stroke his cock. "I mean to ensure you never forget it."

"That would be impossible." He claimed her mouth once more, his tongue driving deep into her as she worked his shaft.

His hips moved, and she responded, arching off the bed. Grazing her hand with his, he too found her sex, his finger sliding into her. Juliana opened her legs and lifted, meeting his thrusts. She was beyond desperate.

Wrapping her legs around his hips, she brought his cock to her sex. Together, they guided him into her. He stroked in deep, clasping her hip.

Lucas brushed her hair back from her face and kissed her forehead. "I can't go slow. Next time."

"Yes please." She didn't want slow or gentle. She wanted to feel him in every part of her.

Digging her heels into his backside, she urged

him to move. He readily complied, his hips snapping against hers. He went fast, filling her over and over and driving her to the edge of her control. She toppled right over that cliff into a wonderful oblivion as his finger rubbed her clitoris, intensifying her orgasm. Crying out, she squeezed around him, her body shuddering with release.

He slowed, maintaining a steady rhythm as she recovered. His mouth found hers, kissing her with a lazy but utterly decadent abandon, rekindling her desire until she was nearly panting with want again.

She clutched at his head and moved beneath him, urging him to increase his speed. Again, he met her needs, driving into her with rapid thrusts until she was crying out again as her body neared completion once more.

Reaching down, she grabbed his backside, digging her fingers into his flesh. He growled her name. Then the world fell apart as she came again. Whimpering with satisfaction, she held him close as he spent himself, his body trembling.

After a few minutes, he rolled to the side, and she moved with him. She didn't intend to let him go tonight. Indeed, she wasn't sure how she was going to let him go come morning.

She put her hand on his chest, feeling his heart thundering, but begin to slow as they caught their breath. "Next time, I'll be on top."

He turned his head. "Is that right?"

"I like to ride. Did I tell you about my horse, Clio? I ride her every day. In fact, I miss her greatly when I'm away."

"So, you're saying you're in need of a good ride." His provocative smile made her heart flip.

"Yes, I'm saying that." She traced her fingertips

around his nipple. "I should warn you that I'm a very good rider. I don't tire easily."

He groaned. "You are, without a doubt, the most astonishing woman I've ever met." He put his arm out to the side and gazed at her in open admiration. "I am yours to command."

~

*J*uliana smiled even before she opened her eyes. What a spectacular night. She would be tired today, but it would be well worth it.

Rolling over, she reached out for Lucas. There was nothing but cold, empty bedclothes. Her eyes shot open, and she scanned the room in search of him.

It was empty.

He'd arisen early yesterday, so he was likely downstairs already. Eager to see him and spend what little time they had left together, she bounded from the bed. She quickly washed and dressed, noticing that his things were also gone. Ah well, he'd probably taken them downstairs since they would be leaving today.

To confirm that, she went to the window. Light clouds grayed the sky, and the snow was mostly gone, leaving mud behind. It would be a slow travel day, but they could leave.

Damn, she'd secretly hoped it would snow again.

After pinning her hair into place, she made her way downstairs. The Garretts were already in the common room, as were a few other guests. Mrs. Lilley was bustling about as usual.

"Good morning," Mrs. Garrett greeted Juliana. "Would you like to join us for breakfast?"

Juliana didn't see Lucas. "I'd enjoy that, thank you. Is his lordship also joining you?"

"We haven't seen him." Mrs. Garrett's attention darted to the left. "Hal, do not taunt your sister!" She glanced back to Juliana. "Excuse me."

Frowning, Juliana went to Mrs. Lilley, who'd just delivered tea to a table. "Begging your pardon, Mrs. Lilley, I wondered if you might know where Lord Audlington is."

The woman stared at her a long, increasingly awkward moment. "Ah, you don't know that he left earlier?"

He'd left without saying anything to her? Juliana's insides crumpled. She felt as if she'd fallen off a moving coach. This was jarring. Unexpected. And it hurt. "No, I didn't know that."

"Oh dear. I'm sorry. You'll have to excuse me for now, but I can help you later." She gave Juliana a warm smile before hurrying toward the kitchen.

Juliana hadn't expected anything from him, but after the night they'd shared, it seemed at least courteous for him to bid her farewell. Instead, he'd run off in the early morning hours without a word. She wasn't exactly angry, just very, very disappointed. But feeling that...*that* made her angry. It had been a long time since a man had affected her. Perhaps that was why it had been so long. It was easier—and better—to lead a life without expectation or disappointment.

Still, she wasn't going to regret this interlude. Lucas had made her feel alive in a way she hadn't for years. She'd be grateful for that even if he had turned out to be a self-involved cad. If anything, he'd given her a gift. Now she could consider future...entanglements. Why not?

Juliana pushed away her negative emotions and

dove into her breakfast. Then, with a newfound determination, she packed her things.

Yes, she'd thank Lucas for reminding her that she was a woman and not just a widow. Well, she would have if he hadn't run away. And that was his loss.

CHAPTER 3

Warwickshire, England, October 1803

*J*uliana had never been to a house party. Certainly not one that had been organized to match couples, whether for marriage or...other activities. She tried to recall the exact wording of the invitation, but it had been delivered orally by someone dispatched by their hosts, Lord and Lady Cosford, and she couldn't remember the exact verbiage.

She was looking forward to seeing Lord and Lady Cosford again, and she hoped she might make a few new friends. More importantly, she hoped to conduct a liaison. The notion filled her with a giddy thrill.

It had been several months since her last assignation, a three-month long affair with Conrad Smithson, a widower who lived in Skipton. He'd proposed marriage, despite her telling him she wasn't interested, so she'd ended their arrangement. Why would she wed when she was financially secure and enjoyed the comfortable independence of widowhood?

This house party provided the perfect opportunity for a limited liaison, just for the duration of the party. For Juliana, it sounded ideal.

Her coach stopped in front of Blickton, the Earl of Cosford's country seat, a magnificent Palladian-fronted house built within the last century. A footman opened the door and helped her down. Immediately, she noted the stiff breeze and the sky darkening in the distance to her left. She hurried into the house.

"Welcome to Blickton," the butler greeted with a bow.

Lady Cosford sailed into the entry hall, a wide smile lighting her features. "Mrs. Sheldon, how lovely to see you. I'm so glad you could finally come to visit."

"I'm so glad you invited me. I'm sorry I wasn't able to attend last year." Juliana had received an invitation to another house party about this time last year, but she'd been committed to helping her friend who'd just had a baby. "And please, you must call me Juliana as you did when I visited before." Though, that had been years ago, when she was still married to Vincent.

"Yes, of course, and you will call me Cecilia. I am so pleased our friendship has been rekindled." She took Juliana's arm. "I'm glad you are here. I did wonder if I'd done something to alienate you when you visited with your husband."

"Not at all," Juliana assured her. "I was somewhat of a hermit those first few years."

Lady Cosford's sherry-brown eyes fixed on her. "What finally brought you out of seclusion?"

Juliana couldn't tell her the truth—that it had

been a surprising tryst with a viscount at an inn during a snowstorm. "I suppose it was just time."

"Well, that's a mysterious answer," Lady Cosford said playfully.

The Mysterious Widow. That's what Lucas had called her.

Cool air breezed against Juliana's back.

Lady Cosford's eyes sparkled as she looked toward the door. "Another guest has arrived. Come, I'll introduce you to Lord Audlington."

Juliana froze, and it had nothing to do with the cold wind that had blustered into the hall, because the door was now closed. Turning slowly, she watched as Lucas handed his hat and gloves to the butler and made small talk.

Oh, this was going to be *good*.

Lady Cosford led her forward. Lucas faced them then, his gaze landing on their hostess first then moving to Juliana. The look in his eyes as recognition bloomed nearly made Juliana cackle with glee. She'd thought never to see him again. She'd certainly never expected to meet him *here*.

That she did so in a way that allowed her to shock him was utterly delicious.

"Audlington, allow me to present my friend, Mrs. Juliana Sheldon."

Lucas bowed deeply. "It is my distinct honor."

Juliana dipped into a shallow curtsey. It was all he deserved.

"Juliana, this is the Viscount Audlington."

Juliana clamped her jaws together lest she correct Cecilia and inform her that he was better known as the Runaway Viscount. At least to Juliana.

"You're the first to arrive," Lady Cosford said to both of them. "We'll be gathering in the drawing room in about an hour, as the majority of the guests will be trickling in around then. In the meantime, I'll have Vernon here show you up to your rooms. As it happens, you're rather near each other."

Juliana avoided looking at Lucas. She didn't want to know what he would think of that. He'd probably want her to invite him to visit her bed, but she would not. She might have come for a liaison, but she was *not* going to conduct it with him.

She did, however, glance toward Cecilia. Had she placed the two of them in close proximity by design? Did she hope for Juliana and Audlington to form an attachment? If so, she would be disappointed.

Cecilia took her arm from Juliana's. "I'll see you soon."

"Yes, thank you." Juliana followed the butler, a fifty-or-so-year-old man of average height with a thick middle and dark gray hair.

Vernon led them up the stairs. "You're both in the west wing."

Lucas whispered, "I had no idea you would be here."

Juliana kept her gaze focused upward as they ascended. "Would you have decided not to come?" she asked coolly. "Never fear, you can always run away. You're quite good at that."

"Run away? I didn't—"

She slid a look toward him and quashed a smile at the consternation pulling at his handsome face. "When you leave a woman in bed without so much as a peck on the cheek, what would you call it?"

"I left you a note!" His voice rose on the last word, drawing Vernon to look back over his shoulder as he reached the gallery at the top of the stairs.

"Where?"

"I gave it to Mr. Lilley. Actually, it wasn't a note. I told him to tell you I decided to leave as soon as possible because it looked like it might rain."

"How...special that makes me feel, your lordship. Unfortunately, Mr. Lilley didn't relay any kind of message whatsoever. The Garrett children were rather disappointed that they didn't get to say goodbye."

He made a sound that was something between a growl and a grunt. It sounded as if he might have hurt himself making it. She hoped so.

Goodness, she hadn't thought she still harbored any anger toward him. Apparently, she'd been wrong.

They walked along the gallery on the first floor until Vernon paused at a door on the left. He opened it for Juliana, but remained in the gallery. "This is yours, Mrs. Sheldon. I understand you did not bring a maid. Lady Cosford has assigned one to you. She will be up shortly, or she may already be in your dressing chamber."

"Thank you." Since Juliana's house was rather small, her lady's maid was also the housekeeper. When Juliana traveled, which was rarely, she left her at home to keep things orderly.

"Yours is at the end, my lord." Vernon continued along the gallery.

"I'll be just a moment," Lucas said.

Vernon paused to look back over his shoulder. "Your room is on the right."

Juliana stood at the threshold of her chamber, and Lucas faced her, saying, "I am very sorry you didn't get my message." He appeared pained.

Trying not to smile at his obvious discomfort, Juliana shrugged. "It hardly signifies. That was nearly two years ago. I hardly remember our time together." This was a brazen lie, but he would never know that.

He stiffened. "I recall it quite distinctly and with great fondness. I shall look forward to rekindling our acquaintance this week."

"Just so long as you understand it will not be the same *kind* of acquaintance." She pressed her lips together and narrowed her eyes. "Have I made myself clear?"

"Abundantly." He leaned close, and she caught his masculine scent of pine and sandalwood. "That will not prevent me from trying to persuade you to forgive me." His striking gray eyes bored into her with promise, and damn it all if she didn't feel a stirring of desire. She'd thought of their tryst often and was even occasionally melancholy that it was just a memory.

That acknowledgment only served to stoke her ire. "Try all you like, my lord. I shall enjoy watching you fail." She stepped back and slammed the door in his face.

Turning, she barely looked at the room's furnishings, her mind racing. This ire she felt toward Lucas was rather surprising. But why would she have expected it? She'd never thought to see him again. Then to encounter him like this... It was a shock. She would become accustomed to his presence, to the fact that he was in her present and not just a figment from her past.

Until then, she would enjoy torturing him. It was the least he deserved.

~

*A*fter dinner that evening, Lucas sat in the dining room sipping port with the other gentlemen at the party. Nervous energy made his foot tap, and he kept glancing in the direction of the drawing room, where the ladies were located.

Where Juliana was located.

She'd sat at the other end of the table at dinner, laughing and conversing with those around her. He didn't think she'd looked his way even once. If she had, she would have seen him trying to win her attention. And why? So he could shout another apology across the dining room that she would almost certainly toss back in his face?

He understood that she was angry. She thought he'd left without saying a word. He would have been upset too.

The truth was that he regretted leaving without seeing her. He'd been anxious to get on the road, to take advantage of the clear weather for as long as it lasted. It was more than that, however. He'd watched her sleeping and seen the potential for a longer dalliance.

Perhaps even a forever dalliance. Which he was fairly certain ought to be marriage.

Only, what if it wasn't forever? What if they were only meant to have a brief liaison, just like all his other affairs? Why would she be different?

Because in the nearly two years since he'd seen her last, since he'd held her in his arms, he'd thought of her more than he'd thought of any woman he'd ever known. Now, she was here, within reach, as if fate wanted them to find each other at the precise moment he'd decided he was ready to marry.

Unfortunately, she did not appear to share his sentiments. It seemed she'd spent the past two years reviling him.

She thought you left without a word!

Even if she had got his message, leaving like

that was still lousy, and he knew it. He needed to make amends. If he could.

Or, he could move on and get to know the other ladies at the party.

Beside him, a gentleman called Howell seemed to read his mind. "Excellent crop of ladies, wouldn't you say?"

"Seems to be." Lucas barely knew the man and wasn't about to discuss prospects with him.

Howell went on. "I'm not necessarily here to wed, mind you, though my daughter could use a mother, I suppose. Hopefully, it will be a grand time either way." He waggled his dark brows. "What about you, Audlington? You're wife hunting, are you not?"

"What makes you say that?"

The older man—he was at least five years Lucas's senior—shrugged. "You're heir to an earldom and of a certain age. I imagine you must be feeling the pressure."

"Excuse me." Annoyed, Lucas stood and moved to an open seat on the other side of the table next to his friend Rotherham. Like Lucas, the earl was here to find a wife, albeit for a different reason. He'd made no secret—at least to Lucas—that he wanted his two daughters to have a mother.

"Something wrong with your former chair?" Roth asked with a slight smile.

"Do you know Howell?" Lucas suspected he did, given Roth's smirk.

"A little. He's harmless." Roth lifted his wine-glass and narrowed his eyes at Lucas over the rim. "He makes you look positively Puritan, however."

Lucas scowled as he settled back in his chair. "My reputation is much improved." He'd been a monk for over a year. Since he'd parted from his mistress, the first—and last—he'd ever taken. It turned out he'd been smart to avoid such entanglements.

"It does seem to be. Your father has finally delivered an edict?"

"Yes, in fact." Lucas was to marry this next Season, or his father would select a wife for him. However, that wasn't the primary motivation driving Lucas, nor would he reveal what it was. His life had...changed. For the first time, he was actually eager to marry and have a family. "I shall hope to find a wife as easily as you did."

"Finding a wife is as easy as you make it. Finding the *right* wife is much more difficult."

Lucas snapped his gaze to his friend, whom he'd met as a young buck. Roth was only three years his senior, but he'd been a guiding influence as Lucas had learned to navigate London. After a few years of extravagance and amusement, Roth's father had died, and Roth had married almost immediately. He'd seemed happy enough, or at least not *un*happy. He'd never indicated displeasure.

"I'm not entirely sure what you're trying to say or if you're trying to impart advice," Lucas said. "If so, please be plain, as I could use all the counsel I can get."

Roth met his eyes. "Don't rush into anything. Just be as certain as you can."

"Is that what you're doing this time around?" Lucas asked quietly.

"I'm bloody well trying." He lifted his glass in mock toast, and Lucas did the same.

"What are you gents plotting?" Sir Godwin Kemp, who was seated on Roth's other side, leaned over to ask. "Laying claim to certain ladies?"

Roth frowned. "That would be rather forward, wouldn't it?"

"What if we're all pursuing the same skirt?" Sir

Godwin laughed heartily while Roth and Lucas just stared at him.

Their host cleared his throat from the head of the table before standing. "I hear snippets of your conversations, and I must ask that we agree to not discuss our...plans for the house party?"

Lord Pritchard, seated next to Cosford, twice widowed and perhaps the most senior gentleman in attendance, approaching his middle forties, said, "You know the ladies are doing the same as we speak."

"That doesn't mean we need to do it too." Cosford looked around the table. "However, I'm sure Lady Cosford would be delighted to know your plans if you care to share them with her privately—or perhaps you already have. I know some of you are hoping to remarry and perhaps your future wife is among us." He smiled broadly. "Nothing would make my wife happier than to help you and the lady of your dreams make a match."

Sir Godwin looked up and down the table, a mischievous glint in his eye. "Any wagers as to whether a marriage proposal results from this party?"

"No wagering," Cosford said a bit crossly. "Lady Cosford was adamant about that. This isn't White's, and we don't have a betting book. Just enjoy yourselves this week, and don't be numskulls. Lady Cosford selected each of you for a reason, and I shall be heartily annoyed if any of you disappoint her."

"We are up to her expectations," Lucas said, casting an expectant look at his fellow gentlemen. "Aren't we?" He raised his glass. "To Lady Cosford and her delightfully...helpful party."

"Hear, hear!" several gentlemen cried. Everyone lifted their port in a toast.

Cosford sat back down, and conversation picked up once more.

Roth cast a surreptitious glance across the table, perhaps at Howell. "I doubt that will stop everyone from at least speculating about other guests."

"People will always whisper amongst themselves," Lucas said. "Just as we are doing." He lifted his lips in a faint smile.

"True," Roth agreed. "I pledge to let you know if there's a lady who catches my eye. That way, you won't steal her from me."

"You think I could do that? You are an earl, and I a mere viscount."

"You *will* be an earl. Plus, you don't have daughters into the bargain."

Lucas didn't have children, at least not any that he could claim. He did, in fact, have a daughter. She was the wonderful product of his arrangement with his short-term mistress, and Lucas had been shocked by how deeply he loved her and how badly he wished he could raise her as his own.

But he would never take her from her mother, so he supported them as best he could, providing for them to live in comfort in Manchester. He forced a smile. "No daughters, just a formerly rakish reputation."

"Bah, that won't prevent anyone from marrying you. You haven't gambled away a fortune or sired a bevy of children."

Not a bevy, no. Lucas gripped the stem of his wineglass and clenched his jaw. "That I have not."

A short while later, they adjourned to join the ladies. The drawing room was situated at the back of the house, with a view of the sweeping parkland. Tonight, however, it was black beyond the windows. The interior sparkled with candles and firelight as well as laughter and conversation.

The women were spread about the room, and furniture had been moved to create space for dancing. A middle-aged woman whom Lucas was certain wasn't a guest moved to the pianoforte while Lord Cosford escorted his wife to the dance floor.

"Attention, if you please," Lord Cosford said loudly. "Lady Cosford has an announcement."

Lady Cosford stood beside him and smiled up at him before addressing the room at large. "Before we begin the dancing, I wanted to share that tomorrow after breakfast, we will have a display of talents. If you have a particular talent you'd like to share, please see me this evening. I am sorry the weather will keep us indoors, but this will be most diverting."

Lucas stifled a groan.

"No talent?" Roth asked with a chuckle.

"None that comes to mind. What the hell are we supposed to do?"

"You could orate. I hear you give a good speech in the Commons."

Lucas snorted. "That would put everyone to sleep. I seem to recall you having a rather nice singing voice."

"For bawdy ballads best sung at a tavern. I doubt Lady Cosford would appreciate such a contribution."

"This is a bawdy house party, is it not?" Lucas laughed, and Roth gave him a good-natured shove.

Lucas scanned the room and spotted Juliana sitting with a few other ladies. "Pardon me, Roth."

Before he could think better of it, he walked to Juliana and summoned his most disarming smile. "Mrs. Sheldon, would you care to dance?"

A look of irritation flashed across her features. Lucas braced himself. "I know it's terribly rude to decline, but I'm afraid I'm a rather poor dancer. I can't seem to move in time to the music. Trust me, your feet will appreciate my refusal." Her responding smile was brittle and rather disingenuous if he had to judge it.

Instead of walking away in defeat, Lucas persisted. He wasn't going to give up that easily. "A promenade, then."

Juliana hesitated, and the woman beside her on the settee—Mrs. Hatcliff-Lind—looked toward her. "You can't decline that too."

"I suppose not." Juliana stood. "Very well."

Before he could offer her his arm, she started toward the door. "Where shall we go since the storm prevents us from walking in the garden?"

"We could just meander through a few rooms," he suggested. Behind them, the music started.

"Or we could fetch a drink from the tray over there in the corner and call it good enough." She flashed another fake smile.

He lowered his voice as he glanced around to ensure no one was near enough to hear them. "I am not giving up until you forgive me. I promise I won't try to seduce you."

"Good, because that would be futile."

"Though, it is my turn, since you seduced me at the Pack Horse."

She sucked in a breath, and he swore there was a flicker of heat in her gaze. "I did not. That was a…mutual seduction."

"Tell yourself that if it helps." He was rather enjoying this now. Rather, he was enjoying the spark of various emotions in her eyes. She appeared to still be affected by him, and he hoped it was in a good way, despite what she said.

"What would be *most* helpful is for you to leave me alone. Do I need to speak with Lord and Lady Cosford?"

He gaped at her. Perhaps she really did loathe him. "And say what?"

"That I don't wish to be around you and that they must do everything possible to keep us apart."

"That's rather childish, isn't it?"

"What's childish is you pestering me after I've said I want nothing to do with you."

That was a direct hit. "I truly hurt you," he said quietly. "I am dreadfully sorry. I should not have left when I did. Not without seeing you." Had their tryst affected her more deeply than he realized? He'd come to think it had left a lasting mark on him. Perhaps it had done the same for her. Perhaps she'd even known that before he'd left, and he'd robbed her of the chance to tell him so.

He wanted to fix this, but he had to accept that doing so might not be possible. At least not the way he wanted things resolved. "If you want me to leave you alone, I will."

"I do." She pivoted toward where the drinks sat on a table.

"If you change your mind, will you let me know?"

"I'll let you work that out," she said sardonically. "Enjoy your evening, my lord."

"You can still call me Lucas," he said to her back.

Well, that had gone worse than he could have imagined. What the hell was he going to do for the rest of the bloody house party? Or for that matter, his life? Seeing Juliana here after all this time had sparked something inside him. And he didn't want to let it die.

CHAPTER 4

*A*fter his frustrating encounter with Juliana the previous evening, Lucas had retreated to the billiards room, where he'd proceeded to drink an inadvisable amount of brandy. He considered skipping the talent exhibition, but decided he didn't want to be the only guest not in attendance.

He did, however, wait to enter the ballroom until the last possible moment. Everyone sat in rows of chairs in front of the dais, where Lady Cosford was already standing. There was an empty chair in the last row next to Roth. Lucas hurriedly slipped into it.

"I thought you might not make it," Roth whispered.

"It was a last-minute surrender." Lucas couldn't help looking for Juliana. She sat beside the dowager Duchess of Kendal.

Lady Cosford introduced the first performer. Lord Satterfield would perform a soliloquy from Hamlet.

"This should be entertaining," Roth said quietly. "He's an excellent orator in the Lords."

Lucas had heard the earl speak and agreed. Indeed, Lord Satterfield's performance was astonishing. He finished to loud applause, which rekindled the ache in Lucas's head.

Lady Cosford returned to the dais to announce the next performer, and Lucas spent the next while trying not to stare at Juliana. There was a song, juggling, a performance on the pianoforte, and then Lady Cosford introduced a poem, which would be recited by Mrs. Juliana Sheldon. Lucas sat up straighter, his gaze fastened on the dais.

Though Juliana was dressed in present-day clothing, her hair was arranged in an old-fashioned style. An elaborate chignon sat high atop the back of her head, and cascades of curls brushed away from her bare forehead, falling over her ears and grazing her cheeks. Seeing an abundance of it down about her face reminded Lucas of when he'd unpinned her hair at the Pack Horse. Hell, he was growing hard just thinking of that.

Roth leaned forward in his chair. "Oh, this will be fun."

"Why do you say that?" Lucas asked.

"Just listen," Roth whispered.

Her eyes met his, and he would have sworn they glittered with a mischievous malice.

She began to speak:

> Amarantha sweet and fair
> Ah braid no more that shining hair!
> As my curious hand or eye
> Hovering round thee let it fly.
>
> Let it fly as unconfin'd
> As its calm ravisher, the wind,
> Who hath left his darling th'East,
> To wanton o'er that spicy nest.

Dear God, she was talking about hair. And

looking at him just often enough to let him know it
was on purpose. Because he adored her hair. She
fingered the curls near her face and slitted her eyes
in a tempting fashion.

> Ev'ry tress must be confest
> But neatly tangled at the best;
> Like a clue of golden thread,
> Most excellently ravelled.

> Do not then wind up that light
> In ribands, and o'er-cloud in night;
> Like the sun in's early ray,
> But shake your head and scatter day.

She lightly caressed her cheek, then swept her
hand down her neck, her touch provocative and
arousing—at least to Lucas. She was torturing him.
Intentionally. He was completely enraptured.

> See 'tis broke! Within this grove
> The bower, and the walks of love,
> Weary lie we down and rest,
> And fan each other's panting breast.

Her hands reached out, her long fingers
searching for an imaginary lover. He realized he
was nearly panting, just as were the couple in the
poem.

> Here we'll strip and cool our fire
> In cream below, in milk-baths higher:

Her green eyes settled on him with a burning
intensity, daring him to look away. He could not.
Holy hell, he was hard as stone. He heard a sharp
indrawn breath from somewhere in front of him,

and realized he was not alone in his reaction. Ridiculously, jealousy surged within him.

> And when all wells are drawn dry,
> I'll drink a tear out of thine eye,

Drawn dry. His mouth was certainly dry. And he wanted to wring another part of himself until it was as barren as the desert. He prayed the poem would be over soon, and yet he never wanted it to end.

> Which our very joys shall leave
> That sorrows thus we can deceive;
> Or our very sorrows weep,
> That joys so ripe, so little keep.

Juliana curtsied, her gaze lingering briefly on Lucas with a look of triumphant glee. She'd chosen this poem quite purposefully—her hair and the man's insistence that they couple now. Except, their tryst had been quite mutual. In fact, she'd been the instigator. Not that he hadn't been a willing and hopeful participant.

Silence had captured the ballroom. No, not quite silence. Lucas fancied he could hear heavy breathing and racing hearts, but how could he hear anything over the raging beat of his own pulse?

Applause erupted at last. Howell got to his feet. "Wonderful! Just wonderful!"

Lucas gritted his teeth. He wanted to inform Howell that the poem hadn't been for him. A quick glance around the rows of chairs seemed to indicate that Howell was not the only one entranced by Juliana's recitation.

"That was brilliant," Roth said. "I can't think of

a better poem to recite at a party such as this, can you?"

Lucas hadn't read much poetry. "I can't think of a poem at all." But this one had likely ruined him for all other poems. Lucas realized Roth was staring at him.

"She's captivated you," Roth said, sounding amazed.

"She's captivated everyone. Even the ladies look breathless."

"It's an arousing piece. You should hear it sung —absolutely sublime." Roth's face lit with a beatific smile. "I daresay Mrs. Sheldon will have several suitors after this."

Lucas scowled.

"You disagree?" Roth asked. "She's beautiful, seems clever, and there's something about her, I think." He looked toward the dais, where Juliana had been joined by Lady Cosford. "An air of self-assurance that's very appealing."

"Are you one of those suitors?" Lucas asked somewhat crossly. He certainly didn't want to compete with one of his closest friends. Especially when that friend was more in want—or need—of a wife than Lucas was. But dammit, Juliana was his. Or had been, anyway.

No, you shared one wonderful night. That doesn't make her yours any more than it made you hers.

"It's a tad early to become attached to one person, I think." Roth glanced at him quickly. "For me, anyway. I must be careful when I wed."

Because he was looking for a mother more than he was a wife. Lucas had told him he should find a woman who would be both, that a companion in parenthood was equally important as one in marriage.

That was something Lucas cared about. He had every intention of being a good parent.

"However, it seems you may want to be at the front of the line for Mrs. Sheldon's attentions."

Lucas considered telling Roth what had happened nearly two years ago, but didn't since the next performer went on to the dais. He watched Juliana take her seat and noted he wasn't the only one following her every movement.

There would be no hope in winning her over now, not when she clearly loathed him and would be fending off advances right and left. It had been a bloody arousing performance. And while it had been for him, her intent was not to satisfy his arousal. It was torment, pure and simple.

He needed to move on. That was going to be deuced hard when he wanted Juliana more than ever.

≈

*J*uliana was keenly aware of how provocative everyone had found her recitation. By the time she'd finished, she'd felt almost breathless. But that was due to how clearly she'd affected one person: the Runaway Viscount.

She'd accomplished her goal, and that was all that mattered. That she now found herself beset by nearly every male guest was her own fault.

Stealing a glance toward Lucas, she saw him standing with the Earl of Rotherham. Lucas darted a look toward her and frowned. Didn't he like that she was garnering so much attention? She knew exactly how next to taunt him.

"Mrs. Sheldon, your recitation was thoroughly

illuminating," Mr. Howell said, moving close to her side.

"Thank you." She fluttered her lashes at him. "I'm so pleased you enjoyed it."

Another gentleman, Mr. Emerson, inclined his head toward her. "Spectacular performance. My favorite, which isn't to say the others weren't also brilliant."

"I appreciate your praise, Mr. Emerson," she said warmly.

From the dais, Lady Cosford announced there would be cards in the drawing room or a tour of the orangery, which meant a quick dash through a potential shower—it had been raining on and off all day—to reach the exterior building.

"Would you care to take me on a tour of the orangery?" she asked Mr. Emerson, noting that Lucas was near the doorway. They'd have to walk right past him.

A brief flicker of surprise flashed in Emerson's eyes, but it was quickly replaced with anticipation. "It would be my pleasure." He offered Juliana his arm.

Of medium height, with broad shoulders, Emerson was about the same age as Juliana. His auburn hair was trimmed in the latest style, and his brown eyes glimmered with intelligence and warmth. Juliana preferred him to Howell, who was more aggressive in his behavior.

Juliana set her hand on his sleeve, and they walked toward the door. As they passed Lucas, Juliana didn't turn her head. She did, however, glance toward him from the side of her eye. He was scowling.

Emerson escorted her from the ballroom. "How did you choose that poem?"

She couldn't very well tell him the truth, that

she'd thought it would provoke Lucas. "It seemed appropriate for this party."

He chuckled. "Indeed it was. I see you matched your hair to the time period when Lovelace wrote the poem."

Touching the back of her head, she nodded, pleased that he'd noticed. "I did."

"Perhaps you'll bring it back into style," he said with a smile as he opened the door to the path that led to the orangery. "We should hurry."

They dashed to the orangery and quickly went inside, where some other guests were already mingling.

Lord Cosford appeared. "You're here for the tour. The orangery isn't terribly large, so it really isn't much of a tour, I'm afraid. You are free to meander amongst the plants we've brought in for the winter. The orange trees are at the other end."

"Shall we investigate the orange trees?" Emerson asked.

"Certainly," Juliana murmured, looking back toward the door to see if Lucas had followed.

Did she want him to? For someone who said she didn't want anything to do with him, she was giving him a great deal of her attention. How much torture would be enough? She wasn't sure, but felt confident she'd know when she reached that point.

Perhaps what she needed was to be distracted by another gentleman. To truly *not* care about Lucas.

As they started toward the orange trees, she heard a husky laugh behind them. Turning her head, she saw that Lucas had arrived. And he wasn't alone. The extremely attractive Mrs. Wynne-Hargest was on his arm. The Welshwoman possessed an abundance of curves along with an alluring face that surely drew men into her orbit with little effort. She was also quite charming and witty. Juliana had liked her as soon as they met. Indeed, Juliana liked all the ladies in attendance.

Still, the sight of her hanging on Lucas's arm and looking up at him with a flirtatious smile made Juliana want to push her aside and take her place. No! She didn't want that. She just wanted his full attention so she could make him miserable.

"Do you know how many orange trees there are?" Juliana asked loudly enough for Lucas to hear. She supposed she wanted him to follow her.

"I do not. We shall find out shortly," Emerson said as they walked amidst the other vegetation. They soon arrived at the other end of the orangery and had their answer. "It looks like six."

"Are there oranges?" This came from Mrs. Wynne-Hargest as she and Lucas arrived behind them. She tugged Lucas toward one of the trees. "I see one."

"Should we pick it?" he asked, his tone light and teasing.

"We should pick it first," Juliana said to Emerson, clutching his arm more tightly as Lucas looked in their direction.

"I'll pick it for you if you like," Emerson responded before adding in a lower tone, "I don't like them, actually. They make my face pucker." He demonstrated, and Juliana's answering laugh was genuine.

"That's not helpful when you're at a party where you might want to, ah, put forth your best face."

He grinned. "My thoughts exactly."

"I think we should leave it," Mrs. Wynne-Hargest said. "This is a tour, not a harvest. Perhaps Lady Cosford has another plan for it. In any case, I'm eager to go play cards. Anyone else?"

Emerson inclined his head. "I am as well."

"Then let us return to the house," Lucas said, pivoting with Mrs. Wynne-Hargest. He sent Juliana a smug look, and she nearly rolled her eyes.

"I shall ask Lady Cosford to ensure we sit together at dinner," Juliana said to Emerson as they followed Lucas and Mrs. Wynne-Hargest back toward the door.

"I should like that very much."

"I'll do the same," Lucas said to Mrs. Wynne-Hargest. "I look forward to deepening our acquaintance."

They left the orangery to find the rain had stopped, so there was no need to hurry to the house.

Juliana gazed longingly toward the park. "I do hope we'll be able to ride soon." She missed her daily rides on Clio.

"You enjoy riding?" Emerson asked.

"I do."

Lucas held the door open for Juliana and Emerson, who thanked him. They continued to the drawing room, but Juliana paused before they went inside. Taking her hand from Emerson's arm, she said, "This is where I leave you. I'm not really in the mood for cards. I hear the library calling my name."

Emerson's brow furrowed. He was clearly disappointed. "That's a shame. Until later, then." He took her hand and dropped a kiss on the back.

"I am breathless with anticipation," Juliana said. She turned and walked to the library without listening to whatever Mrs. Wynne-Hargest and Lucas were saying to one another.

Once in the library, Juliana shook out her shoulders and let out a long exhalation. Perhaps she was behaving badly. Continuing to torment

Lucas was pointless. It was immensely satisfying, however.

"Your poem was most titillating."

Juliana startled, nearly dropping the book she'd just taken from the shelf. Spinning about, she clutched the book to her chest. "You followed me. Again."

Lucas arched a tawny brow. "I wanted to fetch a book."

"And you were overcome with compulsion to tour the orangery?"

He shrugged. "Mrs. Wynne-Hargest was in need of a companion."

"I'm surprised you aren't keeping her company at cards."

He prowled toward her. "I'm surprised you aren't hanging on Emerson after you dragged him to the orangery."

"There was no *dragging*. He was entirely amenable."

"Of course he was. You enraptured everyone with your provocative recitation at the talent exhibition. I doubt anyone would have declined your invitation. I would not have."

"You would not have been invited."

"Can that be true?" He almost smiled. "I was certain you spoke that poem directly to me."

"I did no such thing."

He moved to stand near her, leaning his shoulder against the bookcase. "Liar. You chose a seductive poem about *hair*. Look me in the eye and tell me you weren't thinking of our night at the Pack Horse."

Juliana edged slightly closer to him and snared his gaze. "I was *not* thinking of the Pack Horse. Or *you*." Lies, lies, lies. She was a lying liar. And he knew it.

He studied her a moment, his expression hungry. "This hairstyle you're sporting is magnificent. Your hair is down, yet not. It's absolutely intoxicating. How long do you plan to torture me exactly?"

In that moment, Juliana wondered if she wasn't torturing herself too. If she hadn't been thinking of their tryst when she'd delivered the poem—and she most certainly had—she would be now. Her mind was awash with the memory of his kiss, his touch, his every breath as he worshipped her body.

Then he'd left her without a word.

"I haven't decided yet," she said, lifting her chin. "You deserve a great deal of torment."

He reached to the shelf behind her, bringing his body in front of hers so that they nearly touched. She pressed back against the books even though every fiber of her body wanted to lean into him.

"I do deserve that," he said softly, his lips near her ear. "Please continue. I am beginning to enjoy it."

Pulling a book from the shelf, he backed away from her, leaving her on the edge of panting with desire. At least internally. She worked very hard to keep her body stiff and her features impassive.

His gaze locked with hers, and the satisfied smile curving his lips said she hadn't been entirely successful.

"See you at dinner."

He stalked from the library, whistling a merry tune. Whistling!

Juliana gritted her teeth. How dare he enjoy her taunting?

She would see him at dinner, and she would be ruthless.

*a*s Lucas descended the stairs for dinner, he tried not to think of how close he'd come to kissing Juliana in the library or how he suspected she'd wanted him to. The old rakish version of him would have done it without a second thought. But he was giving her a taste of her own punishment, and judging by the heat in her gaze, he'd found success.

He smiled to himself as he made his way to the dining room. Lady Cosford intercepted him.

"Why, Lord Audlington, you look pleased. I hope that means you're having a good time."

"I am, thank you. You've assembled a delightful group of guests, and your entertainments are unmatched."

She preened a bit. "Thank you. Tomorrow will be *quite* diverting. You won't want to miss a thing."

"What do we have to look forward to?"

Shaking her head, she pressed her lips together briefly. "I'm not divulging my secrets yet. You'll just have to wait and see. In the meantime, I've placed you next to Mrs. Wynne-Hargest at your request. I've also seated you beside Mrs. Dunthorpe, who I believe is interested in marriage. Since I know that is also your objective, I thought you might like to get to know one another."

Lucas felt a wave of disappointment and quickly pushed it away. "She told you that was her intent?"

"No. None of the ladies have confided a desire to wed. Since they are all widows, that is to be expected. However, Mrs. Dunthorpe has a way about her that is endearing and thoughtful. She's an excellent listener, and I daresay she'd make an excellent wife."

"That is good to know," he said with a benign smile.

Lady Cosford lowered her voice and moved closer. "I am rather confident there are at least a few ladies here who would entertain remarriage in the right circumstances. And you, with your courtesy title and forthcoming earldom, are well positioned for such a match." She winked at him.

It sounded so mercenary, and yet he knew this was how marriages often worked. Those with the most to offer often had the greatest success. He'd been the goal of many a matchmaking mama, particularly in his younger days, before his rakish reputation had taken root.

"I do appreciate your support, Lady Cosford. However, I am not certain I'll find my future viscountess here. Nor do I need to. I have an entire Season to find a suitable match." He made it sound so simple, as if he weren't a man of thirty-three who'd squandered plenty of years.

A look of distress became etched into her features. "I hope you aren't saying that because you find everyone wanting."

"Not at all. If I do meet my wife here, I shall be entirely grateful to you and your matchmaking endeavors."

She laughed. "You see right through me. Ah well, I like to see people happy. I do hope you'll enjoy your dinner companions." She gave him a parting smile as she turned to move toward the drawing room, where everyone gathered before dinner.

He'd hoped to spar with Juliana, but she was speaking with Mr. Dryden on the other side of the room.

"Good evening, my lord."

Lucas turned to see Mrs. Wynne-Hargest. The widow's dark eyes glittered as she slowly perused him. It wasn't a blatant invitation, but it was close.

The butler announced dinner, so Lucas offered his arm to Mrs. Wynne-Hargest. She curled her hand around his arm and brushed her breast against his elbow. He suddenly wondered if he'd been too hasty in asking to sit beside her.

Lucas held Mrs. Wynne-Hargest's chair and turned to see Sir Godwin helping Mrs. Dunthorpe into her seat. Lucas bid her good evening as he sat.

Mrs. Dunthorpe was younger than him, perhaps even younger than Juliana. With auburn hair swept into a sleek, elegant style and eyes the color of chocolate, she had an air of self-possession that reminded him of Juliana.

Who was sitting directly across the table from him.

Like him, she was flanked by members of the opposite sex. Emerson and Howell sat on either side of her. They both looked quite pleased to be there. Howell was admiring her bosom, while Emerson was leaning toward her and saying something Lucas couldn't hear. Juliana laughed softly, and Lucas decided it was going to be an interminable meal.

Dammit, he wanted to be sitting beside her,

leaning close, and he wanted to do more than just look at her breasts. He'd held them, kissed them, suckled them until she moaned his name.

Lucas reached for his wine and took a very long drink.

As the first course was served, Mrs. Wynne-Hargest leaned toward him. "Lady Cosford says we're to play a special version of blindman's buff tomorrow."

That must have been the secret to which Lady Cosford had referred. But why did Mrs. Wynne-Hargest know? Likely because women shared things. Didn't they?

He smiled at Mrs. Wynne-Hargest. "What else do you ladies discuss when we aren't around?"

She waved her soup spoon. "All of you, of course. Don't tell me you aren't doing the same. How many wagers have been placed about the outcomes of this party?"

"I honestly don't know. I haven't placed any."

"But some *have* been placed?"

"I couldn't say, but Lord Cosford said we weren't allowed. Are you ladies betting?"

"Certainly not!" She leaned close once more. "Just a little, but you didn't hear that from me, and do *not* inform Lady Cosford. She also told us not to."

"She won't hear it from me." Lucas glanced over at Juliana, who was doing her best to talk with both men on either side of her. "I wouldn't say a word to anyone, especially if you can tell me what's being said about me." In particular, he wanted to know what Juliana was saying, but he wouldn't go that far in his inquiry.

"Are you extorting me for information?" She let out a low, throaty laugh.

"Never," he said blandly. "But perhaps we can

trade intelligence. I can tell you that you are regarded as beautiful and beguiling."

"Spoken like the rake we all know you to be."

"That's who I *used* to be. I'm reformed." He sipped his soup.

She pouted. "How dull. We couldn't quite tell if you were here in search of a wife or if you intended to continue your profligate ways. It seems the former must be true, and I was hoping for the latter."

It sounded as if Juliana hadn't said a word about him. Or if she had, Mrs. Wynne-Hargest hadn't heard it. "Come now, profligate is excessive, don't you think?"

He drank more wine and tried to listen to what was being said across the table.

"I would have called it arousing," Howell said, loud enough so Lucas could make it out.

Juliana laughed softly, but then directed her attention to Emerson. She also stole a glance toward Lucas, saw that he was watching her, and immediately looked away.

He spent the remainder of the course speaking with Mrs. Dunthorpe and eyeing Juliana as much as he dared.

During the next course, Lucas noted Howell leaning closer and closer to Juliana. She became less and less conversational with him until she finally seemed to snap. Turning her head sharply in Howell's direction, she said something rather urgently. Lucas recognized that expression, particularly the lines between her brows—because she'd used it on him at this party: she was aggravated with Howell.

Lucas clutched his wineglass so he wouldn't leap up and grab Howell instead. If he was insulting her in any way, he'd have Lucas to answer to.

Oh hell. Lucas was not her protector. Nor was he her suitor. And he certainly wasn't her betrothed or husband.

Howell paled a shade or two and murmured something. Juliana turned her full attention, which included a dazzling smile that was completely at odds with her prior expression, on Emerson, the lucky chap.

At last, dessert was served, and Lucas felt as though he were nearing the end of a long and arduous race. Riding a goat. Over a mountain. In a snowstorm.

Howell started speaking to Juliana again, but in a quieter, more deferential voice. Whatever she'd said to him had been effective.

"I do hope you'll save me a dance later," Mrs. Wynne-Hargest said, drawing Lucas's attention.

"Of course." He responded without thinking. He didn't particularly want to dance. He wanted to take Howell outside and plant him a facer.

The meal concluded, and the ladies removed to the drawing room. Lucas decided he wasn't going to stay either. Standing, he nearly ran into Roth who'd apparently come from the other end of the table where he'd been sitting.

"I'd thought to join you," Roth said. "You aren't staying?"

"I don't want port." He wanted something stronger. There had to be some whisky about somewhere.

"I'm sure Cosford will ask them to bring whatever you like."

It wasn't just the bloody liquor. "I don't want to stay."

"You seem agitated. Did something happen?"

Only that he'd been a fool and allowed something wonderful to slip through his fingers. "I'll see you later."

Lucas departed, likely causing a stir amongst the gentlemen. Once outside the dining room, he paused, uncertain where to go. His gaze drifted in the direction of the drawing room. Where Juliana would be.

Alas, there wasn't likely to be any whisky there. Furthermore, he'd cause a commotion since the ladies probably expected—and appreciated—their time without having to suffer the men. He turned on his heel and stalked to the library, fairly certain he'd seen a liquor cabinet or at least a tray.

The library was an immense room with soaring shelves bursting with an astonishing collection of books. There were several seating areas about the room, including a few alcoves tucked between the shelves. Lucas thought he'd seen the liquor across from the great fireplace.

Before he could reach his destination, he stopped short, for he was not alone. A flash of green in the far corner caught his eye. Only one lady had been wearing that color tonight.

His feet carried him toward her, and she finally detected his presence, turning from the shelf. Her green eyes, made even more striking by the color of her gown, moved over him, making his breath hitch. "You followed me to the library again."

"Actually, I did not. I was merely trying to escape the dining room and came here in search of whisky. I recalled there was a liquor assortment here."

She inclined her head across the room. "It's over there."

He glanced where she'd indicated. "So it is."

"Why did you wish to escape the dining room?"

"It was that or knock Howell to the ground. I decided this was the safer option."

Her eyes narrowed slightly. "Why would you do that?"

"He was clearly bothering you."

"He was, but I managed him." She looked quite proud of herself.

Lucas couldn't help smiling. "I'm dying to know what you said."

"He kept pressing his thigh against mine, and he had the nerve to put his hand on my knee. I informed him that if he didn't stop, I would use my fork to pierce the back of his hand, his leg, and perhaps other, more…intimate parts of his body. He didn't touch me again."

Laughter erupted from Lucas, and he nearly swept her into his arms for a celebratory kiss. He had to remind himself that they did not have that sort of relationship, no matter how badly he wanted it. Did he want it?

Oh yes. He wanted her any way he could have her. He just wanted to be *with* her. Even when she was tormenting him, he felt more alive than he had in ages. Since he'd seen her last, really. When he'd completely cocked things up.

But how was he to know he'd met the woman who would snare him, body and mind? Perhaps even soul. He hadn't realized it until this very moment. Fate had intervened and brought them together again. He was certain of it.

He sobered, staring at her intently and probably with an obvious hunger. "You are a marvel. I am in awe of your strength and poise."

She arched a brow. "Because I threatened to jab him?"

"Because you are capable, witty, and fiercely passionate—whether you're threatening an overzealous libertine or righteously torturing a discourteous cad."

"I have given you a nickname, and it isn't that. You're the Runaway Viscount." She walked toward the liquor cabinet, and he trailed behind. Not because he was in search of whisky, but because he would have gone anywhere she led him.

"That's rather tame given how you feel about me," he said.

She perused the bottles on the tray atop the cabinet. "It's fitting. How is it you think I feel about you?" Pivoting, she gazed at him with cool expectation. "I don't think there's any whisky."

Lucas was having a hard time focusing on anything but her. She was so damned alluring. Did she have any idea how badly he wanted her, especially when she looked at him as if she wanted to eviscerate him?

He'd called her passionate, and he knew firsthand just how much. He wanted every bit of it directed at him.

Forcing himself to look at the bottles, he made a quick decision and picked one up. "Rum, then."

He poured a glass and handed it to her, then poured one for himself. After taking a generous sip, he boldly asked, "Are you conducting a liaison with Emerson?"

"That's none of your concern." She brought her glass to her lips and took a small sip. Her face creased in reaction.

"Never had rum before?"

"No. But I like trying new things, such as this house party. I'd never been to one. I've also never punished a gentleman for his bad behavior, and I confess that has been most diverting."

"You have more than made your point, but as I said, I am enjoying your attentions. Indeed, I will take them any way I can get them." He took another drink. "If you aren't engaged with another gentleman, might I offer myself?" Whatever happened, at least he'd tried. He couldn't let the opportunity pass.

Her eyes rounded slightly. "You're propositioning me after abandoning me at the Pack Horse nearly two years ago?"

"That's somewhat hyperbolic, isn't it? I made a mistake. I shouldn't have left you like that." He edged forward, closing the gap between them. "I'm beginning to think I never should have left you at all."

"That's absurd."

"I don't think so. I never stopped thinking about you, wondering about you. If we hadn't met at this house party, I might have come to find you in Skipton."

"I can't believe that's true."

"Why not?"

"Because you're a viscount in need of a wife. Doesn't she need to be of certain stock? I'm a bookseller's daughter who married above my station. That I now find myself as a guest of Lord and Lady Cosford is the true absurdity."

Lucas frowned. "It isn't at all. You've every right to be here. Aren't you and Lady Cosford friends?"

"Not close ones."

"I don't think that matters. She invited you, and you've proven yourself to be quite popular."

"Because I recited a provocative poem."

"Perhaps, but I always see people around you. You're interesting and intelligent. You won't convince me that people don't like you for *you*. I certainly do."

She narrowed her eyes, but there was a playful

glimmer in them. "You're just trying to coax me into your bed."

He grinned shamelessly. "Is it working?"

In response, she sipped her rum, her gaze holding his.

"That isn't a no," he whispered, anticipation racing through him. "Whether you believe me or not, you are special to me. We could spend the rest of this house party as we did at the Pack Horse. Tell me that doesn't interest you. Or even arouse you."

She swallowed, and he swore he could see her heartbeat pulsing in her throat. He longed to lick her flesh in that very spot, to stoke the desire he hoped she still felt for him.

"Here they are!" Mrs. Wynne-Hargest announced.

Lucas stepped back from Juliana as she took a longer sip of rum. She also avoided his gaze.

Mrs. Wynne-Hargest came into the library with Lady Clinton. The latter spoke next. "We came to find you to say the dancing is about to begin.

Mrs. Wynne-Hargest walked toward him. "You promised me a dance."

Lucas glanced toward Juliana, whose brows rose. She said nothing. "Mrs. Sheldon and I were just sampling the rum."

"How is it?" Mrs. Wynne-Hargest took the glass from his fingertips and took a sip. She promptly coughed. "My goodness, that's strong." She made a face. "I'll stick to wine, thank you." Setting the glass on the cabinet, she turned to Lucas and curled her hand about his elbow. "Let's go dance."

"Are you coming, Mrs. Sheldon?" Lucas asked, though he was certain he already knew the answer."

Juliana pressed her lips together as if she were

trying not to laugh. "I don't think so. Enjoy yourselves." She lifted her glass in silent toast.

Disappointed but not defeated, Lucas departed
the library with the other ladies. He hoped he'd
made progress with Juliana. The more he thought
about her, the more he realized she *was* special.
After more than ten years of not being at all moved
to wed, he began to imagine what it might be like
to be married.

To her.

Perhaps he should tell her that instead of suggesting another liaison. Especially since she hadn't
bared her claws this time. And most of all because
she hadn't said no.

CHAPTER 6

*A*fter taking an early morning ride, Juliana felt *glorious*. Which was an achievement since she hadn't slept all that well. Blast Lucas and his infernal seductive charm. He'd almost coaxed her into his arms last night in the library. If not for the untimely arrival of Mrs. Wynne-Hargest and Lady Clinton, Juliana would have abandoned her commitment to make him suffer.

Except now she was nearly certain she was suffering too.

He wanted her—that was abundantly clear. It was also now clear—at least to her—that she wanted him too.

Why had he blathered on about her being special? It was likely just a rakish ploy to lure her into his bed. She would not be so weak. No matter how enticing his bed sounded.

"Mrs. Sheldon?"

Juliana jerked from her reverie, recalling that she was in the drawing room, and they were having a group discussion about their objectives for the party. She turned her head to the left, where Mrs. Hatcliff-Lind, who'd spoken her name, sat sharing the settee.

The scent of roses wafted about Juliana as Mrs. Hatcliff-Lind patted her hair. "My apologies, I was woolgathering," Juliana said.

Mrs. Hatcliff-Lind watched her expectantly. "It's your turn to say whether you would remarry."

Right. That had been the topic of conversation, whether any of them would want to wed again. Before she'd fallen into her thoughts, Juliana had heard Mrs. Dunthorpe say she was considering it. That had led Juliana to recall that Mrs. Dunthorpe had been seated next to Lucas at dinner, which had in turn led her to wonder if the viscount had danced with her in addition to Mrs. Wynne-Hargest. Probably.

Why should Juliana care? She didn't even like dancing.

Damn, she was gathering wool again.

"I have no intention to take on another husband," Juliana said. "I'm comfortable as I am." Particularly if she could engage in the occasional affair. As she'd done last spring, and as she'd done with Lucas nearly two years ago.

Mrs. Hatcliff-Lind spoke next. "I'd entertain an offer—for the right price. I suppose I'm comfortable enough, but I've five children and wouldn't turn my nose up at a viscount or an earl." She winked at the room at large and chuckled.

Apparently, she was the last to share her intentions, because Mrs. Wynne-Hargest said, "It seems the majority of us are here for some temporary excitement." Her dark eyes glittered with mirth. "Has anyone found that yet?"

Lady Clinton put her hand to her chest. "*I* certainly wouldn't say."

"Surely we can share amongst ourselves," Mrs. Wynne-Hargest argued. "Can't we all agree that what happens at Blickton stays at Blickton?"

There were nods in response, but no one said anything.

Mrs. Wynne-Hargest exhaled and threw up her hands. "Fine. If it means anything, I have nothing to share, but I would have if I did. Indeed, I hope to find…engagement soon and will keep you apprised." She arched her brows and grinned.

Juliana was confident the woman was referring to Lucas. She clenched her teeth so she wouldn't tell Mrs. Wynne-Hargest to keep her hands to herself.

Except she couldn't be jealous of the attention other women gave Lucas when she could very well have him as her own. He'd openly stated that they could repeat their tryst from the Pack Horse. He'd also spouted nonsense about searching for her in Skipton. To what end? He certainly wasn't going to marry her. Nor did she want to wed for the reason she'd stated a few minutes ago. She'd already turned down one proposal this year.

Lady Cosford appeared in the doorway, rescuing Juliana from her thoughts. "It's time for blindman's buff in the ballroom."

Juliana rose along with everyone else and moved to the ballroom. Lady Cosford stood on the dais. She looked out over the guests and nodded toward each one as if she were counting. "If I have my sums correct, everyone is here. As you know, we're going to play blindman's buff. Does anyone *not* know how to play?

Everyone looked about, but no one answered. "Excellent," Lady Cosford said. "We're going to add a little something to our game today. When the blind man—or woman—finds and correctly identifies a person, he or she will kiss them."

This garnered some responses, though they

weren't loud enough for Juliana to hear. There was also laughter.

Sir Godwin cleared his throat. "What if I pick Lord Audlington?" His gaze moved to his left and landed on Lucas. Impeccably garbed, with a smile teasing his mouth, Lucas was breathtakingly handsome.

On the dais, Lady Cosford answered, "You may kiss him however you like—there are no rules as to the type of kiss."

Sir Godwin cocked his head. "How about as soon as I realize I've found a gentleman, I purposely lose so I can try again?" This garnered more laughter.

"That is entirely your prerogative," Lady Cosford said. "You may also choose to watch instead of play."

To Juliana's right, the dowager Duchess of Kendal indicated she'd be watching, as did Mr. Sterling, who stood beside her. He escorted the dowager to the chairs assembled near the wall.

"Anyone else?" Lady Cosford asked loudly, pausing for anyone to respond.

Juliana's gaze darted to Lucas. He was watching her, of course. There was a glint of promise and confidence in his gaze, as if he were assuring her that he would be the one to find her.

Not if I find you first.

Did she want to find him?

Of course she did. Then she could kiss him, which she realized she wanted very badly to do, under the auspices of playing a game.

Weren't they playing a game anyway? She hadn't thought so until last night perhaps. Until he'd decided he was enjoying her punishment. That had changed the rules.

It was time to change them again. She only hoped she'd be able to pick him out.

A slow smile pulled her lips up as she realized what else she'd be able to do—if she were chosen, she'd kiss someone *before* she kissed him. Meaning, she'd have the chance to torment him just a little more.

"Let's get started, then!" Lady Cosford announced. "Remember, you can't move after the person is blindfolded, else they'll never find anyone." A small table sat atop the dais holding a bowl filled with pieces of parchment. She plucked a piece of paper and unfolded it before reading aloud, "Lord Satterfield!"

Lord Cosford came forth and blindfolded the earl, then spun him about. Satterfield grumbled about being dizzy and then thrust his arms out as he attempted to find someone. Then he'd have to correctly identify them in order to kiss them. Or, in a regular version of the game, pass on the blindfold to whomever he'd found and named.

After much flailing, he found Mrs. Makepeace and managed to correctly identify her. They exchanged a few words, which Juliana couldn't hear before the earl dropped a rather chaste kiss upon her lips.

Juliana slid a glance toward Lucas. He was watching Mrs. Makepeace try to find her way like a drunken sailor after she'd been blindfolded and spun about. She weaved toward Juliana, who thought kissing Mrs. Makepeace might rival the Lovelace poem in terms of provocation.

In the end, Mrs. Makepeace grabbed Juliana's arm and moved her hand up to Juliana's capped sleeve. "I can tell this is a woman. Can I just keep looking, please?"

Laughter sounded, and Lady Cosford said, "Yes,

go ahead. Perhaps we should have the women move aside for now?"

Lady Clinton called out, "What if I *want* to kiss Mrs. Makepeace?"

Mr. Emerson grinned. "I say we let her."

Eventually, Mrs. Makepeace chose Lord Pritchard and gave him a kiss on the cheek. With the difference in their ages—probably twenty years—she looked as if she were bussing her father.

The game continued, and after a few more rounds, Juliana began to grow frustrated that neither she nor Lucas had been caught. Judging from the way his brow creased more deeply with each new blind man, she suspected he felt the same way.

At last, Emerson stumbled into Juliana. "Let me see…I did pay attention to where everyone was standing, and this must be Mrs. Sheldon."

"You are correct," she said with a smile, thinking this couldn't have gone any better. Of all the men for her to kiss in order to torture Lucas, Emerson was perfect.

He pulled off the blindfold, and Juliana gave him a coy stare with a light shrug. Anticipation flashed in his eyes just before he lowered his head. Juliana put her hand on his chest and leaned in, meeting his lips with her own.

The kiss was brief but decidedly unchaste as their lips had been parted. Juliana retreated slowly, letting her fingertips sweep down his lapel a few inches as her gaze held his.

Then she spun about. "My turn."

Just before the blindfold slipped over her eyes, she found Lucas. His jaw was tight, and the set of his features advertised one word: intent.

If she wanted to be extra cruel, she could choose someone else. No, this was never about being cruel. She'd been angry, but it *had* turned into a game. The question now was who would win.

Emerson spun her in merciless circles, making her quite dizzy so that she had to clutch his arm briefly lest she fall to the floor. "All right?" he asked softly.

"Yes, thank you." Where the hell was Lucas?

Juliana worked to regain her bearings, but the blindfold allowed nothing, not even light so she could ascertain the location of the windows. She relied on her other senses, particularly scent—she knew exactly what Lucas smelled like.

Inhaling as she made her way, she caught the strong scent of roses. That was Mrs. Hatcliff-Lind. And she was on the opposite side of the room from Lucas. Pivoting, Juliana put her arms out and started her search in earnest, careful not to stalk directly to where she thought Lucas was standing.

She came close to someone, but she wasn't sure it was Lucas. Damn, this was harder than it looked. She inhaled deeply and couldn't smell pine or sandalwood. Continuing to her left, she kept her hands up and prayed she wouldn't accidentally hit someone else, for then she'd have to guess until she discovered their identity.

A sound reached her ears—the barest clearing of a throat. It could be nothing or it could be Lucas signaling her. Moving in that direction, she kept up her sniffing strategy. Finally, she was rewarded with a familiar masculine scent.

She touched his chest, pressing both hands against him and moving her hands up his coat toward his shoulders. "I think... I think this is Lord Audlington."

"Finally," he muttered so only she could hear.

"Well done!" someone said from behind her.

Juliana untied the blindfold and clutched it in

her hand. She met Lucas's smoldering gaze and nearly melted.

"You shouldn't have kissed Emerson like that," he whispered as she moved closer to him, nearly pressing her chest to his.

"Why not? That's the game."

He clasped her waist in a decidedly possessive manner. "Because you rather stoked my jealousy, and now I feel a primal urgency to show everyone here that you are *mine*."

"Do your worst, my lord." She stood on her toes and kissed him. As with Emerson, her lips were parted—so were Lucas's. But this wasn't brief or even slightly chaste. It was erotic and soul stirring, his tongue sliding along hers as he cupped the side of her neck.

His thumb stroked her jawline, and she was utterly lost. Curling her fingers into his coat, she stifled a moan as lust careened through her.

A cough sounded nearby, and Juliana recalled they were in a ballroom at a house party surrounded by a great many people who were most assuredly watching them.

He realized it too, for he released her and stepped back. She did the same, putting distance between them, which was the exact opposite of what she wanted to do.

After what seemed an eternity, Lady Cosford said, "I think it's time for refreshments!"

People moved toward the table with drinks and food. But Juliana strode to a chair where she deposited the blindfold. Then she looked back at Lucas over her shoulder and left the ballroom.

～

*L*ucas's heart thundered as his vision tunneled after Juliana. He was already hard as granite, but the sultry look she'd given him crushed the last of his defenses. Not that he was trying overly hard to resist her.

Had that been an invitation for him to follow? He wasn't going to wait to find out.

He hastened after her, leaving the ballroom without a second thought. Where would she go?

Upstairs? That was where *he* wanted to go. Her chamber, his, he didn't care. Since he seemed to always find her in the library, he ought to go there.

He walked in that direction and caught a flash of yellow—the color of her dress—in the staircase hall. Veering left, he strode into the hall just as she was starting up the stairs. He practically ran to catch up with her.

"I thought you might go to the library," he said as he came up behind her on the stairs.

"Is that where you'd rather go?" she asked, pausing. "There's hardly any privacy."

"There are a few alcoves. I tupped a widow in an alcove at a ball when I was twenty."

She narrowed her eyes. "Do you think I want to hear about your past exploits? Don't make me change my mind."

He moved onto her stair. "I didn't particularly enjoy seeing you kiss Emerson. And that was *today*, not thirteen years ago."

Leaning toward him, she gave him a coy look. "Did that bother you?"

"You damn well know it did. Why else would you do it?"

She shrugged and ascended to the landing halfway up, where the staircase turned left. "I didn't kiss him the way I kissed you."

Growling, Lucas clasped her waist and drove her backward to the wall, pressing her against the wood with his body. "I'm glad, because I would have had to hit him."

"That would have been incredibly inappropriate." She slid her hand up his chest and twined it around his neck, pulling his head down at the precise moment he moved in to kiss her.

"But wholly necessary." His mouth claimed hers, their lips and tongues wildly mating as he thrust his hips against hers.

She gasped, breaking the kiss. "Why? You can't go around committing violence on my behalf."

He cupped her chin, holding her as he stared into her eyes. "Because you are mine. Whether you realize it or not. And I want—no, I *need*—everyone at this bloody party to know that."

"If you keep kissing me on the stairs, I daresay they will."

With another growl, he kissed her again, this time quickly, using his teeth to pull on her lower lip just before he swept her into his arms and hurried up the stairs.

"Lucas!" she hissed. "This isn't at all discreet!"

"The hell with discretion."

He carried her directly to her chamber, but couldn't open the door without setting her down. Swearing softly, he lowered her to the floor. She opened the door and held it for him.

He stepped over the threshold and barely pushed the door closed before she leapt on him. She pushed his coat from his shoulders in a frenzy.

They tore at each other's clothing, sailing garment after garment to the floor until she stood before him in her chemise and garters. She raked her gaze over him. "Those boots have to go."

"Yes." He sat on the edge of the bed and pulled them off. Then his stockings followed.

Juliana moved between his legs and placed her hands on his chest, her fingertips grazing his nipples. Desire arced through him, and he gripped her waist before sliding his hands up her back.

Bending her head, she kissed the hollow of his throat, swirling her tongue against his skin. He plucked at the pins in her hair, dropping them to the floor without care. As the thick mass fell, he tangled his fingers in the satiny strands.

He inhaled her evocative scent. "God, your hair is amazing. I've dreamed of your hair. When you recited that damned poem, I thought I might burst."

"That was my intent," she murmured, kissing his chest and moving her hand down to unbutton his fall.

"You're a siren. Luring me close and then punishing me."

She lifted her head and looked into his eyes. "Did you hate it?"

He cupped her nape, digging his fingers into her flesh, claiming her. "I loved every moment." Pulling her to him, he kissed her deeply, using his mouth to banish any doubt she might have about how badly he wanted her, how desperate she made him.

When his fall was loose, she slid her hand into his breeches and encircled his cock. She stroked him slowly, repeatedly, driving him almost instantly to the brink of release.

He grabbed her wrist and broke their kiss. "Stop. Or I'm going to come all over your hand." He grimaced as she arched her brow. "I haven't been with a woman in over a year."

Her hand stilled. "Poor man. I was without a

man for, let me see, nearly *five* years when I met you at the Pack Horse. Did I complain about that?" She was still torturing him, and he couldn't help laughing.

"Fair enough. And now?" He hadn't meant to ask, but he was suddenly curious if she'd been with another man since they'd met.

"It's been several months, but I'm quite adept at satisfying myself." She resumed her stroking and scored her fingernails along his balls. "It seems you are not."

"Your hand and my hand are not the same. I will never be able to satisfy myself the way you can. It's not the same for you?"

"I do prefer someone else's attentions." She leaned forward and licked the outer rim of his ear. "And if I'm being honest, I liked yours best."

Lucas moaned as he worked not to spend himself in her hand. *"Temptress."*

She pushed him back on the bed and pulled at his breeches, tugging them over his hips and down his legs. Her head bent at his waist. "Shall I take you in my mouth?"

"I won't last." But what a wonderful way to go.

She chuckled, and the sound was unbelievably arousing. "Try." She clasped the base of his sex with one hand and pulled back the foreskin to suckle the tip.

He thrust up, filling her mouth. She took him deep so that he nudged the back of her throat. He gripped the bedclothes to keep himself from tumbling into the abyss.

Gripping his hip, she held his cock and moved her mouth over him, establishing an erotic rhythm where they gave and took with increasing speed. Lucas tugged at her hair and murmured her name over and over. Now, he really was going to come.

"Unless you want me to spill myself in your mouth, you need to stop."

She pulled away and looked up at him. "Do you want me to?"

"I want you to ride me like your bloody horse."

Heat sparked in her eyes, and she reached down to grasp the hem of her chemise. She pulled the garment up over her body, revealing her flesh inch by tantalizing inch. His hands itched to cup her breasts, to pull her down so he could take her into his mouth. She moved to untie one of her garters.

"Leave them," he growled, scooting back onto the bed and turning so that his legs were atop it.

She climbed on after him and straddled his thighs. Now he put his hands on her, caressing her breasts and tugging on her nipples. She arched her back, thrusting herself more fully into his touch. "Harder."

He squeezed her flesh, pinching until she moaned, her hips moving over him in wild abandon. "You are a goddess."

Clasping his cock once more, she positioned herself over him and guided him into her wet channel. Lucas cast his head back and groaned as she pressed down, taking him deep.

Holding her hips, his fingertips dug into her soft backside as she began to move. She indeed rode him like her horse, as she'd ridden him at the Pack Horse, her thighs gliding against his in a delicious and primal rhythm.

She fell forward and kissed him, their tongues clashing. Lifting her head, she put her hands on his shoulders, bracing herself as her movements became more frenzied. He captured her nipple in his mouth, suckling hard, then put his hand between them to stroke her clitoris.

She cried out, rising completely to straighten

her spine as she moved hard and fast over him. Her muscles squeezed him as her orgasm racked her body. He was close to coming, his balls tightening as he thrust into her in deep, rapid strokes.

Fuck. He needed to pull out. He didn't always bother—he hadn't when they'd conducted their tryst at the Pack Horse—but things had changed.

He pulled her off him and put his hand around his cock to finish. White lights sparked behind his eyelids as he came. Her hand joined his, and she stroked him until his body quieted.

"You didn't have to do that," she said, taking her hand away.

"I thought it was necessary," he muttered, trying to reclaim his equilibrium.

"I told you it's unlikely I can get with child." She lay on her side next to him. "Why is it that you bothered to leave me this time and not before?"

"I must have been overcome by you at the Pack Horse." He flashed her a smile as he sat up and went to tidy up at the washstand.

"It seemed like you were overcome today too," she said, also rising from the bed. "But perhaps with marriage looming in your mind, you are more cognizant of creating a child. Just know that you needn't worry about that with me."

He supposed that was convenient. Except hadn't he begun to think that he might want to marry her? Did it matter that she couldn't have children?

"You're certain you can't carry?" he asked.

She joined him at the washstand and cleaned up while he moved back to the bed. "I told you that Vincent and I were quite amorous at the start of our marriage. I was disappointed when I didn't get with child, but I learned to accept that I couldn't change that."

"It could be to do with him, though," Lucas said, sliding into the bedclothes.

"Perhaps, but I had an affair last spring for a few months, and there wasn't a child then either." She lifted a shoulder. "I've accepted that I won't be a mother. I will say, it has made my life rather simple." She turned to the bed. "I take it children are important to you?"

He held the covers for her as she slipped between them. "Yes." He'd had no idea how much until recently. Taking a wife who likely couldn't bear them gave him pause, which he loathed. He cared for Juliana a great deal and had begun to imagine a future with her. A future in which she tormented him, and he adored every moment of it.

She lay on her side facing him. "You should probably not spend this house party carrying on with me, then. Your future viscountess may be downstairs."

"I doubt that. If they aren't already pairing us off after that kiss during blindman's buff, they will be once they've noticed we both disappeared."

She exhaled. "Probably. My apologies. I know you wish to wed."

"There is always next Season." How depressing that sounded. "I detest the Marriage Mart." Wedding Juliana would mean he could avoid it entirely. "Will you marry again?"

She shook her head. "I don't think so. I'm quite comfortable in my current situation. Besides, I didn't enjoy it as much as I expected to. You know that after a few years, my marriage became entirely platonic. Indeed, more often than not, we frayed each other's nerves."

He propped his head on his hand, staking his elbow into the mattress. "How so?"

"I wanted to know about the estate, but he

didn't like to discuss it with me. I wanted to entertain more often, but he didn't like having people at the house. My parents only visited twice during my entire marriage."

"That sounds terribly dull." He couldn't see her enjoying that at all. "Not all marriages are like that."

"I know. My parents are quite happy and deeply in love." Juliana brushed her hair back from her face and lifted her head to pull the mass to the side. "But I think that's rare. My siblings are also wed, and while they are happy, I'm not sure either would describe their relationships as lasting love affairs."

"I believe I mentioned that my parents are like yours," Lucas said. "And so is my brother's union."

"Your brother was about to have a baby last time I saw you. Did everything turn out all right?"

Lucas smiled, thinking of his nephew. "Yes, Daniel is a precocious thing. They are expecting another child in the spring."

"How wonderful. I can hear the envy in your voice," she said.

"Perhaps." They were disgustingly content. Perhaps Lucas *was* a tad envious. He didn't want to think about them or the discussion he was just having with Juliana. He preferred to contemplate the next few days with her. He reached for a lock of her hair, wrapping it around his forefinger. "May I interpret this encounter to mean this can continue?"

"I don't see why not." She scooted toward him and touched his jaw with her fingertips. "But, I just want to enjoy our time here at the house party. I don't want to look to the future or the past. And I will have no regrets when it's over. Can you promise the same?"

"I can." But he wouldn't. He would never stop thinking of the tryst that had brought them together nearly two years ago, and he couldn't stop himself from dreaming of the future. He leaned forward and kissed her, then ran his thumb over her lips.

She sucked it into her mouth, and he groaned softly.

He pushed her back and moved over her. "All I'm thinking of in this moment is having you in my arms."

CHAPTER 7

*T*he following day, it was nice enough in the afternoon for everyone to walk to the river. At first, Juliana and Lucas had thought not to spend every moment of the party together, but that sentiment had quickly vanished at dinner the night before. They'd been seated side by side, likely because of their kiss during blindman's buff and subsequent disappearance. Despite their efforts to behave as if they were only friends, they'd ended up brushing hands beneath the table a countless number of times.

Juliana was fairly certain that everyone was aware of their affair, particularly since he'd spent the night in her room, which no one knew for certain, and they'd also sat together at breakfast, which everyone knew.

So, as the guests gathered to walk to the river, Lucas offered her his arm and murmured, "We may as well."

Laughing softly, she clutched his elbow. "Let's hang back, though. That way, I won't be self-conscious of people staring at us."

"They can stare at Sir Godwin and Mrs.

Fitzwarren instead," he said. "We're yesterday's news already."

It did seem that way. The other guests had cast their surreptitious looks and sly smiles toward Juliana and Lucas last night, but this morning at breakfast, everyone had been more interested in Sir Godwin and Mrs. Fitzwarren, who'd sat together. Now, they walked with their arms linked and heads bent close together.

"I confess I'm glad to have attention on them instead of us. I want you to be able to leave this party without lingering speculation. You have a viscountess to find."

His muscles tensed briefly. "I don't mind the speculation."

"You wouldn't. You're a rake." She squeezed his arm. "My apologies, *used* to be a rake."

"Tease me all you like. I'm ready to settle down. You, however, have swept me away, and there is no one I would rather be with. Indeed, I don't think anything or anyone could tear me away from you." He looked over at her, and she couldn't ignore the way her heart seized or her insides melted.

But then she thought about what he'd said— there was no one he would rather be with, and nothing could tear him away. That sounded as if he wanted something permanent.

She diverted the conversation to more present matters. "It's nice to be outside finally. We seem to always be cooped up when we're together."

He grinned. "You're right. First at the Pack Horse with the snow and now here with the rain. Upon consideration, I am actually quite grateful for poor weather."

The group stopped up ahead. Lord Cosford turned to face everyone and spoke loudly. "Behind that copse of trees, there is a folly. If you'd like to take a detour to investigate it, please do so. However, be advised that the path is not graveled like this one. It will likely be muddy from the rain." Cosford smiled. "We'll be sure to visit it tomorrow when we take our ride. Onward to the river!" He turned and continued leading them along the path.

Lucas paused when they reached the fork. "Should we?" he asked with a mischievous smile that carried more than a hint of heat.

Juliana's body reacted, her nipples hardening in anticipation of what they might get up to. "No one else went. It seems we must."

"What about the mud?"

"I'm game to get dirty." She gave him a sultry look and pulled him onto the nongraveled path.

They circuited the copse of trees and came upon a small folly created to look like a dilapidated temple. Even the foliage around it was made to look wild, as if it were overgrowing the building. However, it looked neatly maintained. That didn't spoil its allure. "This is new since I was here last," Juliana noted.

"Yes, I think Cosford built it perhaps three or four years ago."

She surveyed the columns, two of which had been crafted to appear crumbled and as if they'd fallen down. "It's quaint."

"It's an excellent spot for a tryst." Lucas pulled her behind the folly, where there was a solid wall. There was also a stone that had supposedly tumbled from the top of the temple. "I'm shocked Sir Godwin and Mrs. Fitzwarren didn't take the bait."

"They may on the return, so we should probably be quick." Juliana turned into him and slid her hand around his waist.

Lucas cupped her neck and kissed her hungrily, mirroring the desperate need she felt for him. Just five minutes ago, she'd been enjoying their pleasant, pastoral stroll. But then he'd invited her to this folly with that look in his eye, and she could think of nothing but unbuttoning his fall and guiding his rigid cock into her ready sheath.

He brought his hand down over her breast, but there was a frustrating amount of clothing separating them. She moaned, and he guided her backward a step.

"Put your foot on the stone." He used his teeth to remove the glove from his right hand, then cast it aside, while she did what he said and braced her boot on the somewhat flat top of the rock.

He quickly tossed up her skirt and skimmed his fingertips along her thigh before sliding one into her sex. Juliana grasped his lapels and pulled him toward her. They almost toppled backward, but he caught her around the waist with his free hand.

She kissed him while he pleasured her, his thumb swirling her clitoris with increasing speed and insistence. It wasn't enough, even with two of his fingers thrusting into her. She wanted him to fill her completely, to drive into her with raw savagery.

"You make me a wanton," she rasped, breaking the kiss as she reached down to unbutton his fall.

"You make me wild and desperate. I can't ever get enough of you." He kissed her neck, nipping her flesh.

She reached into his clothing and freed his cock. But she still wore a glove, which made her rather ineffectual. "It's very hard to stroke you without a bare hand," she said with annoyance.

He pressed against her, fixing her skirt at her waist between them. "Put me inside you. Now."

His hand joined hers, and together, they guided him into her. He moved to grasp her thigh, pulling it up around his hip. Then he thrust deep, holding her steady as she balanced on one foot. She felt the wall against her spine as he eased her back gently.

"All right?" he asked.

"More than. Please move."

He licked her ear. "Like this?" He circled his hips against hers, grinding into her.

Juliana gasped, closing her eyes against the sunlight. "No, not like that. In and out, hard and fast. This is not the time or place to tease me, Lucas."

"God, I love hearing my name on your lips." He kissed her, ravaging her mouth while he continued to move slowly with shallow strokes. At last, he drove into her. "Is that better?"

Her muscles clenched, hungry for release. "Not fast enough. I want to come. Don't you?"

"I'm nearly there." He quickened his pace, his mouth against her throat as her orgasm stole over her. She cried out his name, careful not to be too loud.

She felt him tense. He let out a low, guttural sound as he came. Digging her fingers into his coat, she rode him through the sweet bliss of her climax.

When they were spent, he carefully unhooked her leg from his waist. She used her chemise to tidy herself and watched as he whipped a handkerchief from his pocket so he could do the same.

"Did you bring that just for this purpose?"

He arched a brow at her. "One must always be prepared.

She laughed, and he tucked himself away before rebuttoning his fall. Then he bent to retrieve his glove.

"That was quite divine." He brushed his mouth over hers, and her desire stirred once more.

Would she always be this aroused by him? It reminded her somewhat of when she'd met Vincent, and that cooled her ardor.

Except he wasn't Vincent. Lucas pursued her with a relentless passion and joy, as well as with humor and consideration. He'd put up with her "punishment," and she believed he was truly regretful about his past behavior. And here he was postponing his marriage plans. Because of her. That made her feel simultaneously thrilled and uncomfortable. Despite the way she'd treated him upon seeing him again, she didn't want to hurt him. Nor did she want to be hurt—as she had been when he'd left her at the inn.

The sound of voices nearby made Juliana freeze. Her gaze met that of Lucas, who brought his finger to his lips, then pulled her back against the folly.

"This will do," a lady said from inside the folly. "Don't you think so, Winnie?"

Juliana mouthed the name "Winnie" in question just as Lucas did the same. She had to press her hand over her mouth to keep from laughing.

A low moan carried on the air. It had to be Sir Godwin and Mrs. Fitzwarren. Or another lady with Sir Godwin. Who else would Winnie be? Juliana couldn't think of another guest for whom that nickname would apply.

Lucas inclined his head and took her hand. They crept around the folly to the path, moving quickly so as not to attract the attention of the lovers inside the folly. Although Juliana suspected it would be rather difficult to interrupt their activities.

When they reached the main path, they finally exhaled. "That could have been very awkward," Lucas said with a laugh.

She took his arm as they turned toward the

river. "Should we go back to the house instead? To avoid any looks or comments?"

"It's up to you. I am enjoying being outside. Furthermore, I don't care what anyone says or thinks." He looked over at her. "I only care what you think. I am entirely focused on you. Besotted, actually." His tone was light, and he'd returned his attention to the path in front of them, but Juliana couldn't ignore the word *besotted*.

"You do know what besotted means?"

"I do," he said, sounding amused. "And I have no apologies for feeling that way. Can you say you feel nothing for me but a rampant lust? I'm afraid that bit is obvious." He winked at her.

Juliana smiled in response instead of considering his question, for that was more complicated than she wanted their attachment to be. "You are far too charming. Stop it."

"So you can't say it. Good. Because I think you should reconsider marrying again. In fact, I think you should consider marrying me."

Because he was smiling and they were walking, she rather thought he was joking. Perhaps that was because she wanted it to be nothing more than a jest. She decided not to take him seriously. "You know I cannot. You need an heir, and you won't get one from me."

"Don't forget that I have a brother, and he already has an heir with a potential spare on the way." His tone remained light, and now she really did wonder if he was serious or not.

She was thankfully spared having to continue the conversation as they arrived at the river where tables with refreshments were set up, including a special ale that Cosford's brewer had crafted just for the party.

A footman poured ale for them, and Lucas

handed her a small tankard. As they drank, Lord Pritchard approached to have his refilled.

"Capital day," Pritchard said, lifting his mug before taking a drink.

"It's lovely to be out," Juliana said.

Pritchard looked to Lucas. "I haven't had a chance to tell you that I appreciated your speech on the military service amendment. I happened to be near the chamber that day and wanted to hear it. Very passionately delivered."

"Thank you. I'm glad the amendment passed."

"Cheers." Pritchard helped himself to a small sandwich before ambling back toward a group of guests near the river.

Juliana looked at Lucas over the rim of her tankard. "Do you serve in the Commons now?"

Lucas nodded. "Since last year. I wanted to do something more worthwhile, and anyway, someday I'll take my father's seat in the Lords."

"What speech did you give?"

"We'd just passed a bill requiring counties draft lists of men that would need to report to compulsory training. It didn't make sense to me when we already have so many volunteers. The amendment allows the king to suspend the requirements if he deems the number of volunteers to be high enough."

"That sounds reasonable," Juliana said. "You're a passionate orator, then? Why doesn't that surprise me?" she murmured.

Lucas's eyes glinted with humor. "I don't really like to do anything without full commitment."

So Juliana was gathering. He seemed quite committed to their liaison.

Lord and Lady Cosford came to join them. After a few minutes of idle chatter, Lady Cosford moved closer to Juliana and spoke quietly. "How did you find the folly?"

Their hostess was one of the most observant people Juliana had ever met. She suspected Lady Cosford was quite aware of everything going on at the party. "It's charming."

"I'm so pleased. I do hope you're having a nice time."

"I am, thank you." Juliana's gaze drifted briefly to Lucas. "I am so glad you invited me."

"You two seem...enamored of each other," Lady Cosford observed in a whisper while her husband and Lucas conversed about the ale.

"Do we?" Juliana wasn't going to confirm a thing, especially when she was feeling rather confused at the moment. It was hard not to be when Lucas told her he was besotted and suggested she ought to marry him.

Would she wed him if she thought she could bear children? Juliana refused to allow her mind to travel that path. It didn't matter because she couldn't have children, and he needed an heir.

They had this time together, and she would cherish it. She would not contemplate a future, nor would she become besotted—or anything close to that—with him. She'd done both of those things with Vincent, and none of their passion had lasted.

Again, she reminded herself that Lucas wasn't Vincent, that what they shared went beyond the physical. She liked Lucas, which wasn't something she would have said about Vincent.

"I don't mean to pry," Lady Cosford said with a gentle smile. "It is in my nature to try to see that people find happiness. I must remember that does not always mean marriage."

No, it did not. And in this case, Juliana was sorry it wouldn't be lasting.

～

*L*ucas ought to have been exhausted after another night spent with Juliana where sleep had not been their priority. Add to that the long ride they'd all taken that morning, and he wondered why he wasn't sound asleep in his bed. Instead, he felt absolutely exhilarated.

Many of the guests were resting, but after taking a bath, Lucas made his way downstairs to the billiards room, where he found Roth frowning into a glass of brandy.

"What's amiss?" Lucas asked as he went to pour some for himself.

"Nothing, really. Just not making much progress at this party, unlike you and Sir Godwin. And perhaps Satterfield."

"Satterfield has found a match?"

Roth shrugged. "I've just noticed the way he looks at the dowager duchess. I think he'd *like* to make a match, but I can't tell how she feels."

This sounded somewhat like Lucas and Juliana. They'd made a temporary match, but he was coming to realize he wanted more. The more time he spent with her, the more he agonized about parting from her when the party ended.

"Are your sights still on Mrs. Dunthorpe and Mrs. Makepeace?"

"I think I've decided Mrs. Makepeace is too young. Or perhaps it's that I've enjoyed my conversations with Mrs. Dunthorpe more."

"Why is that?"

"She has an excellent eye for fashion and possesses a keen intelligence. She speaks French and likes geography."

"She sounds like she'd be an excellent mother," Lucas murmured.

Roth sent him a beleaguered glance. "Yes, and you know that's what I'm looking for—mostly."

"I'd say entirely, but I'm glad to hear you say that," Lucas said. "I hope you're able to find someone you love. You deserve that." Roth had hoped to fall in love with his wife, but she hadn't wanted that kind of marriage, something she hadn't disclosed until after they'd wed.

"Is that what's happening with you?" Roth asked. "Are you in love with Mrs. Sheldon?"

Lucas wasn't sure he was ready to commit to that, but he'd told her yesterday that he was besotted, and he'd meant it. "Do you remember the tryst I had during that snowstorm two years ago after the new year?"

"Yes, you were trapped at an inn, if I remember correctly. What about it?"

"That was Juliana. Ah, Mrs. Sheldon, I mean."

Roth's eyes widened. "You don't say." He frowned suddenly. "Didn't you regret leaving her at the inn?"

Lucas exhaled. "I did. I never stopped thinking about her." Not even when he'd taken a mistress a few months later. He couldn't imagine doing that now. Not that he would. No, he would take a wife instead.

He suddenly felt queasy. Tossing the brandy down his throat, he poured another.

"What's that about?" Roth asked.

"I think that might be what's happening," Lucas said quietly, clutching his glass. "To answer your earlier question."

"Oh. Well. Does she feel the same?"

"I don't think so." Lucas realized that was the source of his anxiety that was making his stomach roil. "She's content as a widow."

"And you want to make her your viscountess."

"I think I do."

"Please be cautious," Roth said sternly. "Don't make the mistake I did. Be very clear about what you want. What you expect."

"Would you really not have wed Sarah if she'd told you she was only marrying you for security and position?"

"No, I would not." Roth sipped his brandy. "Since you are already falling for Mrs. Sheldon, and you think she doesn't reciprocate your feelings, you should probably sort this out sooner rather than later."

"I can't be in love with her," Lucas decided. "I spent a very short time with her two years ago, and it's only been a few days since we became reacquainted." It just didn't make sense that he would feel so passionately about her so quickly.

Except he did. He wanted to be with her every moment. Even now, he was desperate to see her.

"Have you ever felt this way before?" Roth asked. "I've known you for many years, and I don't recall ever seeing you so...giddy."

Lucas laughed. "What the hell does that mean?"

"There's a bounce in your step, and you seem constantly on the verge of a grin—if you aren't already smiling. Then there's the matter of how often you are in Mrs. Sheldon's company and the things that happen. Kissing her as you did during blindman's buff and then disappearing afterward. Then vanishing again yesterday during the promenade to the river."

"We weren't the only ones," Lucas said, though that wasn't any sort of rational defense or explanation. "So everyone can see I'm a besotted fool?"

"I don't think that's how you appear. You just seem...happy."

"I am, and no, I don't think I've ever felt this

way before." Except when he'd met his week-old daughter. The first moment he'd held Alicia in his arms, he'd felt a love so pure and true that it had made his chest ache. That had been the happiest day of his life.

Lord Pritchard strolled into the billiards room. "The whist tournament is starting shortly, if you're interested." He moved toward the sideboard, and Lucas and Roth stepped aside. "Had to come in here for the brandy, which I see you're drinking. It's the best in the house." He poured what was left in the bottle into a fresh glass. "I do hope there's more of it. Cheers!" He raised his glass and took a drink before striding from the room.

"I suppose I'll play whist," Roth said.

"You don't sound enthusiastic," Lucas observed.

"We're leaving day after tomorrow, so if I'm to determine if Mrs. Dunthorpe would be an acceptable countess, I must get on with it." He finished the rest of his brandy and set the empty glass on the sideboard.

"Acceptable... That sounds rather dull. After your last marriage, I truly hope you can find a thrilling, passionate countess. Doesn't that sound more appealing?"

"Has anyone ever told you that you're too romantically minded?"

"This from a gentleman who was gravely disappointed by the emotional frigidity of his wife. I'd say it takes a romantically minded chap to recognize another one." Lucas chuckled.

Roth shook his head. "You coming?"

"I'll go with you and see if I want to play."

"You mean, you'll look for Mrs. Sheldon, and if she isn't there, you'll decline." Roth snorted. "You're incredibly transparent."

Lucas gave him a sardonic stare. "Apparently, I must bare my soul to her."

"You'll thank me."

"Unless she runs away horrified."

Roth laughed. "If that happens, there's something you're not telling me."

They left the billiards room, and upon arriving for the whist tournament, Lucas saw that Juliana was not present. She was likely in her room or the library.

"Just be forthright about your expectations." Roth clapped Lucas's shoulder before heading into the drawing room.

Lucas turned and went to the library. At first glance, she didn't seem to be there either. Disappointment curled through him, but he knew it would be short-lived. He'd find her. He started to turn.

"Lucas?"

Whipping back around, he scanned the library once more. Juliana poked her head from one of the alcoves along the right side of the room.

Lucas made his way to her, his disappointment forgotten. "I didn't see you there."

The alcove, between two bookcases, contained a cushioned bench on which Julian was curled with a book.

"It's almost private," she said with a slight smile. "Almost."

"Everyone is playing whist. I daresay we'll have all the privacy we want."

She closed the book she was reading on her forefinger. "Are you suggesting something scandalous?" She looked so regal with her gorgeous hair styled atop her head, a pearl comb nestled in the dark curls. The ivory-and-peach gown draping her looked like a delicious confection.

Lucas licked his lips as his body roared into full arousal. "I can't seem to be in your presence without wanting you most fiercely. And when I am not in your presence, I am plotting how to rectify that."

"Is your desire all that motivates you?" she asked, turning toward him and sliding her feet to the floor.

"Not entirely, no. My desire for you is not confined to the physical. I am eager to just be with you." He sat down beside her. "If you're concerned that I am only drawn to you because of our attraction, you must know it's more than that." He'd only just begun to realize how *much* more.

"I am not concerned, actually. I shouldn't have asked," she said rather breezily. "We are conducting an affair, so it is both right and expected that we are driven by our physical desire."

He angled himself toward her on the bench and had to slide his hand under his thigh to keep from touching her. "I feel I must be honest and tell you that I am moved by far more than the physical when it comes to you. When I think of this party ending the day after tomorrow, I am nearly despondent."

"This from the Runaway Viscount who had no compunction about abandoning me."

He heard the humor in her voice but wondered if she still harbored any hurt. Perhaps she always would. He gave up trying not to touch her and took her free hand in his. "I regret that more than anything I've ever done. And I don't want to repeat that mistake. I'd rather not 'run away' at all. I've begun to think we could have more than a temporary liaison."

She stiffened, her hand freezing in his. Then

she withdrew it. "I've told you—I am content as I am. You need to find a wife, and that won't be me."

"But I want it to be you. I've never felt this way about anyone. I believe we could be very happy together."

She gave him a tremulous smile and cupped his cheek. "You will find the right woman, and she will be very lucky."

"Why won't you consider a future with me?"

"I've told you that I can't have children. That should be enough to convince you. I've also explained that I like my life as it is. Furthermore, your wife should be someone from the aristocracy, shouldn't she?"

His suspicion that she did not reciprocate his feelings seemed accurate. Damn, he hadn't expected how sharply that would hurt. "Do you feel nothing for me, then? Beyond the physical."

"I do care for you, but I will not be your wife."

"Not even if I declare my love for you?"

Her jaw seemed to clench. "Not even then. I hope you will respect my decision."

"Of course. But I am still disappointed." He reached for her, intending to cup her chin, but dropped his hand back to his lap. "If it matters, I don't care that you aren't from an aristocratic family, nor am I bothered by whether you can have children or not."

He was surprised to find this was true. After Alicia had been born, he'd wanted so desperately to keep her. Could he really accept a life without children? He looked at Juliana and knew he could. Love was what he wanted, what he'd been running away from.

Surprise flashed in her gaze. "You aren't?"

"I know we can be happy." And at some point— if she agreed to marry him—he'd tell her about his daughter. He'd never shared her existence with anyone.

Her features tightened. "I wish I shared your optimism."

Without it, they couldn't make a future together. He stood. "I didn't mean to pressure you. Forgive me. My parents had a love match, as did my brother, and you've made me certain I want that too. I thought, I'd *hoped*, you and I might make that match. Good afternoon." He inclined his head and left the library.

Instead of retreating to his room or some other uninhabited place in the house, he strode toward the drawing room. If he appeared at the whist tournament without Juliana, the others would note his presence and her absence. They'd speculate as to whether their affair was over, which it was.

Pain cut through him, but he rose above it. He wouldn't wallow, at least not here. There would be plenty of time to lick his wounds after the party at Roth's hunting lodge.

CHAPTER 8

*J*uliana didn't seek out Lady Cosford to request that she and Lucas not be seated next to each other at dinner. She hadn't wanted to draw attention to their separation. Or perhaps she'd just wanted to be near him at least one more time.

That had been a mistake.

The dinner had passed slowly and painfully as they worked to avoid speaking to one another. She didn't think he'd even looked in her direction for more than a fleeting moment. At the end, she couldn't leave the dining room quickly enough.

However, before she could escape to the library or her bedchamber, Lady Cosford swooped in and pulled her aside on the way to the drawing room. The conversation had been short.

Lady Cosford looked at her in distress. "What's happened between you and Audlington?"

Juliana wasn't about to share details. "Nothing."

Frowning, Lady Cosford had persisted. "It is clear that things between you have dramatically cooled—and quickly too. I'm sorry to see it."

"Don't be." Juliana gave her a bright smile. "I think you're aware that the viscount is seeking a wife. I am not, however, in the market for a husband. We simply do not suit."

"Oh." Lady Cosford looked crestfallen, as if she had some sort of personal investment in Juliana and Lucas's relationship.

"Don't be sad," Juliana said. "I'm not. Come, let's go to the drawing room."

She hadn't really wanted to go, but she felt she had to demonstrate that she was still in high spirits. If Lady Cosford had noticed their behavior at dinner, everyone else would have too.

That meant suffering the ladies' curiosity. Juliana drank her first glass of sherry very quickly and immediately asked the footman for a refill. She purposely sat in a chair on the periphery of the room.

Lady Bradford, a dowager countess in her early thirties with three daughters, took the nearest chair and sipped her sherry. "Hard to believe the party is nearly over," she said conversationally.

"Mmm." Juliana sipped her second glass more slowly. She realized it would be better if she could direct the conversation. "Have you enjoyed yourself?"

The dowager nodded. "More than I anticipated actually. You?"

"The same, I think. This is not my typical entertainment. I feel slightly out of my element with all of you."

"You mustn't. Here, we are all friends of the Cosfords, and they are such a delightful couple. They would only associate with the loveliest people, ergo, we are all worthy and wonderful."

Juliana laughed softly. "What a positive outlook."

"I try. I'm sorry that it looks as though you and Lord Audlington have fallen out."

Tensing, Juliana tried to appear nonchalant. "Does it?"

Lady Bradford waved her free hand. "I don't mean to be intrusive. Forgive me."

The dowager was probably around the same age as Lucas. And she was clearly able to produce children. That they were all girls so far didn't mean she couldn't give him an heir. "The viscount is a thoroughly charming gentleman," Juliana said. "He's in the market for a wife, if that interests you."

"It didn't interest you, I take it?"

Juliana shook her head with a slight smile. "I'm comfortably settled."

"And no desire to be a mother?" Lady Bradford took a drink of her sherry. "It's difficult, I confess, but then I have three girls who are very close in age and tend to band together against me. They seem to think they are bordering on adulthood, but they most certainly are *not*," she added wryly. "All that is to say, I understand not wanting to bother with children." Faint color stained her round cheeks. "Goodness, that makes me sound a bit cold. I adore my girls. Truly."

An uncomfortable ache spread in Juliana's gut. She hadn't thought she missed being a mother—it just wasn't something she'd contemplated too deeply after failing to conceive. Why torture oneself with what couldn't be?

She realized she was trying to adopt the same attitude regarding Lucas. Why torture herself with feeling emotion for him when there was no future for them?

Not wanting to endure the torment didn't mean the emotion wasn't there. It *was* there, lurking in the shadows. Just as it had been nearly two years ago when they'd met. She'd tried to shrug away the hurt of him leaving or at least to bury it deeply.

She was afraid to acknowledge her true feelings, let alone embrace them. Perhaps she was the Runaway Widow.

Forcing a weak smile, she said, "Your daughters are lucky to have you. Please excuse me."

Juliana left the drawing room without a backward glance. Thoughts jumbled in her mind, and her throat felt thick. She didn't even stop at the library. Instead, she went up to her bedchamber.

There, she finished the rest of her sherry and set the empty glass on the desk. Perhaps she could ring for a bottle. That would surely keep the emotions at bay.

He wanted to marry her!

She'd come to this party seeking a liaison, never expecting she'd encounter the man who'd broken her heart nearly two years earlier. Broken her heart? What nonsense was that?

Or was it?

Even if she hadn't fallen in love with him at the Pack Horse, and she wasn't sure she had, she'd felt *something*. She'd been smitten with how he'd treated the Garretts—giving them his room and likely paying for it, allowing himself to be a snowball target for their children. His subsequent abandonment hadn't fit the man she'd briefly come to know.

She'd brushed it away as if it hadn't hurt, as if it *couldn't* hurt her. Hadn't she been doing that since her marriage to Vincent had failed to live up to her expectations? What would happen if she surrendered to how she really felt about Lucas? Was she ready to admit she'd fallen in love?

None of that mattered. She had no reason to believe a marriage to him wouldn't end up like her disappointing marriage to Vincent. Furthermore, she couldn't give Lucas an heir, and he would certainly grow to resent that.

Oh, it's far easier and less painful to convince yourself of these things instead of facing the truth, isn't it?

A dark sob startled her. She realized the sound had come from her own mouth. She clapped her shaking hand over her lips.

At some point, she'd decided it was better not to hope for anything, whether it was love or happiness or motherhood, because then she couldn't be hurt or disappointed. And no, she had no guarantee that any risk would pay off—her marriage was evidence of that.

Instead of ringing for sherry, Juliana went to sit by the fire. It didn't warm her, nor did she expect it to. A cold emptiness had settled into her bones, and she doubted it would dissipate.

The maid who'd been assigned to Juliana came into the chamber. "Oh! I didn't realize you were here. I was going to prepare the bed. Do you require assistance?"

Juliana supposed the young woman could help her disrobe. "If you don't mind." She rose from the chair, her limbs wooden as she made her way toward her dressing area.

The maid was quiet while she divested Juliana of her evening gown and underclothes. While Juliana donned her nightclothes, the maid went to turn down the bed. Then she stoked the fire.

Feeling rather ineffectual and generally pathetic, Juliana frowned. This was not like her. She'd never wallowed. Not when she'd realized her marriage was a failure, and certainly not when Vincent had died.

She'd also never let herself truly feel. Perhaps it was time she finally allowed that.

"Fine," she grumbled as if she were capitulating to an invisible force.

"What's that, ma'am?" the maid asked, turning from the fireplace.

"Nothing." Juliana gave her a vague smile. "Thank you for your assistance."

After the maid left, Juliana went to the fire and held out her hands. She *could* warm the chill inside her, and she would. Mayhap she would even seek help. There was one person who knew precisely how to heat every part of her.

She looked to the clock on the mantel. It was probably too early for Lucas to return to his room, but that didn't mean she couldn't go and wait for him.

Emboldened to embrace her emotions, she turned and stalked to the door. She froze just before she opened it. Was this what she truly wanted? To come into the light and admit what she felt for Lucas?

If she waited, the party would be over, and they would go their separate ways again. Except hadn't he said he'd been thinking of going to Skipton to see her? Perhaps he'd pursue her.

No. She'd been clear in her rejection of him. She couldn't expect he would seek another refusal.

This was her move to make.

Juliana slowly opened the door and looked to make sure no one was around. Moving quickly, she made her way to Lucas's chamber. She pushed open the door without knocking and stepped inside.

His chamber was larger than hers and included a separate dressing room. She supposed that was because he was a viscount.

"Good evening, my lord." The masculine voice came from the dressing room doorway just as the valet passed through it. His dark eyes widened upon seeing Juliana. "You are not his lordship."

"No. Are you expecting him?"

"He sent word that he wished to retire early." The man, a few years younger than Juliana, frowned. "I thought you were him arriving."

She smiled warmly. "I'll just wait for him." She'd almost added, "if you don't mind," but didn't want a reason to leave. She was staying until she'd said what she needed to.

Before she could move to the seating area near the fireplace, the door opened behind her. She turned to see Lucas staring at her in surprise. "Juliana."

"I hope you don't mind that I came to speak with you. I was just telling your valet that I planned to wait."

Lucas continued to stare at her, murmuring, "I see." At length, he looked toward his valet. "Thank you, Welton. I can manage."

The valet inclined his head, then went back into the dressing chamber.

"He's staying?" Juliana asked, thinking she didn't want to bare her soul in front of the stranger.

"There's a door that leads to the servants' stairs," Lucas said. Moving past her, he went to peer into the dressing chamber. "He's gone." Turning to face her, he frowned. "Why are you here? I can't imagine what else we have to say."

Had he really given up so easily?

Wasn't that what she'd wanted him to do?

Taking a deep breath, she walked slowly toward him. "I came to tell you that I was..." She hesitated. "No, I *am* afraid."

His brow furrowed. "Of what?"

She stopped in front of him where he stood in

the doorway to the dressing chamber. "That marrying you will end up being like when I married Vincent. That you'll resent the fact that I can't give you an heir. That loving you and inevitably losing you will hurt unbearably." Her heart pounded as though she'd run up three flights of stairs.

Again, he stared at her, his shock evident. He opened his mouth, then closed it again. Then he pulled her into his arms and kissed her. Joy coursed through her. She put her hands on his chest, then slid them up to his neck. How could she have turned her back on this? On him?

Lucas broke the kiss and looked into her eyes. "You love me? Because I love you. Desperately."

"I do. I didn't want to. I *tried* not to."

"Because you're afraid." He caressed her cheek. "You aren't going to lose me. Please don't worry I'll leave you again. I absolutely will not."

She believed him, just as she believed he'd tried to leave her a message. "I know. I just… What if this isn't real?"

He continued to look at her, his gaze intense. "I refuse to consider that. Nothing has ever felt more genuine to me than the love I have for you."

"Will you still feel that way when I don't give you an heir?" She whispered the question, anxiety clogging her throat.

He cupped her face. "My dearest love. I will feel that way until the end of time. I can't express to you how strongly you've affected me, how deeply I care for you. If your husband spoke to you in this manner only to fall out of love, don't tell me. I can't believe it would be possible."

"He didn't. Nor did I tell him that I loved him. We said things such as 'I adore you' or 'you make me so happy' but love was never expressed." Probably because it had never been felt. She brought her hands up his neck, pressing her palms against the skin above his collar. "When I came upstairs, I realized I couldn't be without you. More importantly, I came to acknowledge my trepidation. I didn't think I could risk my heart, but it was either that or allow it to be irreparably broken."

"I promise to guard your heart with all that I am. Will you entrust it to me and be my wife?"

Juliana let out a stuttering breath as her chest swelled. "Yes."

Laughing, he picked her up and turned in a circle before setting her back down and kissing her once more. "You have made me the happiest man alive. I was going to leave in the morning. I couldn't bear to be near you knowing we would have to part."

"I'm sorry I put you through that. And I can't promise I won't worry that this will be fleeting."

"It won't. I *will* promise you that."

She didn't think he could, but appreciated that he wanted to. Comparing him with Vincent wasn't fair, and she wouldn't do it again. Good heavens, she was going to be a viscountess. "I don't know a thing about the peerage."

He lifted a shoulder. "You know me. Rather well, I would say."

"But what about your parents? Your brother? What if they don't like me? What if Society hates me?" Oh God, she was going to have to spend the Season in London. Her soon-to-be husband was a bloody member of Parliament! There would likely be all manner of social requirements.

Juliana began to feel overwhelmed. She broke from his embrace and wove her way to perch on the edge of his bed.

He came to her and knelt down, taking her hand in his. "My family will love you as much as I do." He tipped his head from side to side. "Perhaps *not* that much, which is for the best. My parents will be overjoyed that I am getting married. You could be a potted tree, and they would be equally delighted."

Juliana laughed. "Well, that's not particularly flattering."

He grimaced, then shook his head. "No, it wasn't. I only mean that who you are won't be as important as the fact that you just *are*, that I have finally found love at last."

"Love...not just a wife?"

"The latter was a requirement, but the former is what they hoped for, I think. I really can't wait for you to meet them. And my brother and his wife."

She hoped her introduction to them would go as smoothly as he thought it would. "I admit I'm feeling overwhelmed."

"Once you meet my mother, you will be instantly relieved. She will guide you in any way you ask. And Society will be in awe of your sophistication and wit. I've no doubt you will be a wonderful viscountess. Indeed, I've never before met anyone I wanted to have that role. It seems I was waiting for you to perfectly fill it."

She laughed again. "Now, *that's* flattery. What are you doing down there anyway?" She tugged at his hand. "Can't you see I'm ready for bed? And you're wearing far too many clothes."

"I *can* see that," he said silkily as he trailed his free hand up her bare leg under her dressing gown and night rail. His hand stroked the inside of her knee, then her thigh, making her gasp softly. He went farther still, and she parted her legs for his exploration. When he reached her sex, he stroked along her flesh, dipping the tip of his finger into her. "And I can feel you are wet. Hmm, down here suddenly seems the perfect place for me to be." He released her hand. "I think both hands are required. As well as my mouth."

He pushed her clothing up, and she hurriedly unfastened her dressing gown, then drew her arms from the garment. By then, her night rail was at her waist, and he'd pushed her thighs apart to expose her sex.

Juliana tangled her hand in his hair. "Do your worst."

He put his head between her legs, his breath caressing and arousing her. "On the contrary, my love, I'm going to give you my absolute best."

CHAPTER 9

After escorting Juliana back to her room just before dawn, Lucas had lain awake in his bed, too happy to sleep. He couldn't quite believe that he was betrothed. Actually, it was more that he couldn't believe he'd fallen in love at last. And that he was loved in return.

This was what he'd grown up seeing—his parents' love. Then his brother had fallen hopelessly in love with his wife. Lucas was certain it wouldn't happen for him. He supposed he, like Juliana, had also been afraid. His family's success with love and marriage was a great deal to live up to.

He looked forward to introducing Juliana to them. First, however, they would visit her parents so he could meet them, then they would fetch her horse and other belongings from her home in Skipton, as well as make arrangements for the rest of her things to be sent to Northwich. Once there, she would meet his family and, most importantly of all, the banns would be read.

As much as he'd tried to reassure Juliana about becoming his wife, he had to admit he was a trifle nervous about his father's reaction. His mother would be overjoyed that he'd fallen in love, but his father was likely holding out hope Lucas would marry someone advantageous, such as the Marquess of Hartley's daughter, whom he'd been pushing for for months now. She was more than ten years younger than Lucas and apparently afraid of her own shadow. Or so Lucas's sister-in-law, who knew the young lady's sister, had said.

There was one way to ensure his father welcomed Juliana with open arms. Lucas could tell him about Alicia. He'd be so upset that Lucas had sired an illegitimate child, something he'd warned Lucas against since he'd judged him a profligate more than a decade earlier, that he'd find solace in the fact that Lucas was at least getting married.

Welton finished with Lucas's cravat and stepped back. "You look like a man ready to announce his betrothal, my lord."

Lucas had informed Welton of his news that morning when the valet had come to prepare him for breakfast. "Thank you. And I appreciate your discretion regarding how Mrs. Sheldon and I have spent our nights during the course of the party."

"I've not said a word, my lord, though I have been asked." The valet winked as he tidied up the dressing chamber.

"Which is why you are a marvelous valet." Lucas clapped him on the shoulder before taking his leave. Whistling softly, he made his way to Juliana's room.

Upon arriving, he rapped on her door and fell silent as a smile stole across his lips. She greeted him with a smile of her own. "Good morning. You look more rested than I know you to be."

Lucas's smiled widened. "Joy will do that, I think. I *feel* more rested than I ought to."

Juliana yawned. "I do not. I barely slept after I

returned to my room." She closed the door and took his arm.

They moved toward the stairs. "I didn't sleep a wink," he said cheerfully. "Too giddy."

"Well, we will get plenty of sleep when we visit my parents, because we will not be sharing a bed."

"I can still steal into your room," he whispered, leaning close to her ear.

She shot him a wide-eyed look. "Absolutely not under my parents' noses! You must behave. Or I'll make you stay at an inn."

"That's no fun." He sighed as they reached the bottom of the stairs.

Pausing, Juliana turned slightly toward him. "Do you know what would be fun? If we allowed Lord and Lady Cosford to announce the betrothal. It turns out their matchmaking party was a grand success."

"What an inspired idea. Let's go tell them."

They found their hosts outside the dining room and drew them aside to share the news. Lady Cosford was absolutely delighted. "Another match!" she declared.

Lucas and Juliana exchanged looks of surprise.

"Did someone else become betrothed?" Juliana asked.

"Not this year, but the Duke of Warrington found his bride here last autumn." Lady Cosford grinned. "They are a splendid match, and I did so hope they would attend this year, but they just welcomed their first child."

Cosford looked to Lucas. "You truly want me to announce your betrothal?"

"We do," Lucas said, glancing toward his beautiful wife-to-be.

"Then let us get to it!" Cosford said, gesturing

for them to precede he and Lady Cosford into the dining room.

As Lucas escorted Juliana into the dining room, conversation began to dim. Then it picked back up, perhaps even louder than before. After filling their plates at the sideboard, Lucas and Juliana went to the table and sat together. Over the next quarter hour or so, the rest of the guests filtered in, and it seemed this breakfast was to be fully attended.

When everyone was seated, Cosford arched a brow at Lucas and mouthed, "Now?" Lucas nodded.

Cosford stood at the head of the table. "It's my pleasure to make an announcement this morning." Looking to his left, he smiled at Lucas and Juliana. "It is my distinct honor to share the engagement of Lord Audlington and Mrs. Sheldon!"

Lucas took Juliana's hand beneath the table and gave her a squeeze. She beamed at him, and he wondered how each moment could keep getting better and better.

Applause and cheers rose up around the table. Rotherham lifted his glass of ale. "A toast to the betrothed couple!"

Everyone raised their glasses and called, "Huzzah!"

Several ladies jumped up and moved to swarm Juliana. The gentlemen at the table passed money between them as wagers were settled, prompting Cosford to frown.

After several minutes, things began to quiet, and Lucas and Juliana went to fetch their breakfast. "That was quite a reception," Lucas mused. "Did the women make any wagers as to who would become betrothed?"

"Oh, yes. They will settle their debts later."

"The men were not so covert," Lucas said.

They took their seats, together, and a few minutes later, a footman entered with glasses of champagne on a tray, which he distributed around the table. The conversation amplified once more, and Juliana blushed. "This is very kind of Cosford," she said.

Lucas handed her a glass before taking his own. Their host stood at the head of the table and smiled directly at them. Lifting his glass, he said, "Let us drink a toast to the Viscount Audlington and his future viscountess!"

"Huzzah!"

"Hear, hear!"

Everyone lifted their glasses and drink. This was followed by several more toasts, and the glasses were quickly empty. The footmen hurried to refill them.

When the toasts concluded, Cosford stood again to announce there would be a picnic that afternoon followed by the ball that would officially conclude the party. "One final note. I did request there would be no wagering regarding the romantic outcomes of this party. Clearly, that request was ignored. I implore you to conduct further business privately." He rolled his eyes in a rather pronounced fashion, then sipped his champagne before taking his seat.

"You don't think he's really angry?" Juliana asked.

Lucas shook his head. "Not at all. But the men could take direction from the ladies—the better part of valor is discretion."

As breakfast progressed, Lucas thought of the future with Juliana, of them enjoying breakfast and starting each day together. During the Season, they would live at his house in London, but what about other times of the year? Northwich Hall was large, but she might like her own home to manage. His father owned several estates, one of which Lucas's younger brother lived in with his growing family.

Lucas glanced over at Juliana. Could she really not have children? It would be extremely arrogant of him to think he could father children with her when other men had not. And he knew he *could* have children…

An image of his daughter rose in his mind. He'd seen her exactly twice since her birth the previous spring.

He needed to tell Juliana about her—and he would. As soon as they left the party tomorrow. He hoped she would understand his need to see Alicia at least twice yearly, which was what he and Caroline, her mother, had agreed upon, as well as his promise to always care for them. He paid for their house in Manchester as well as for a nurse and housekeeper to help.

Once he and Juliana were wed, he'd write to Caroline and ask if he could bring Juliana to meet Alicia. He looked forward to that introduction and hoped Juliana might come to love Alicia as he did.

"Lucas?" Juliana said his name softly, her gaze inquisitive as she pulled him from his reverie. "Where did you go?"

"Thinking about our wonderful future," he said, almost wishing the house party would be over today instead of tomorrow. "I can hardly wait for it to start."

∾

*J*uliana stretched as she sat up in bed, her limbs delightfully tired after romping in her bed with Lucas until the middle of the night. They would have tomorrow night at an inn before they reached her parents' house in Leeds the day after that. He'd insisted they would lodge as Lord and Lady Audlington. She hadn't argued.

The maid entered a few minutes later. She came directly to the bedside and bade Juliana good morning. "I've a note for you." She handed Juliana a folded piece of parchment.

Opening the missive, Juliana scanned the brief and clearly hastily drafted communication.

My dearest,

I am so sorry to leave you again, but I must see to a dire emergency. I promise I am not abandoning you and will explain all when we are together again. Know that I love you. I'll come to you in Skipton as soon as I am able.

Yours,

Lucas

He'd left her *again*?

At least this time he'd taken care to write a note. But without explanation. What on earth was so dire that he had to leave without seeing her and couldn't explain? Was someone in his family ill? Surely, he could have said so. What wasn't he telling her? Why hadn't he told her where he'd gone? And why was he planning to meet her in Skipton instead of Leeds, which was where they'd planned to go next? Perhaps he didn't want to meet her parents after all. Because he'd changed his mind. Was he going to cry off?

Frustration and anger battled with worry as she suffered through her toilet. As soon as she was ready, she hurried downstairs and found Cecilia in the dining room. Summoning a brittle smile, Juliana asked their hostess if she could have a word.

"Of course." Cecilia rose from the table and led Juliana from the dining room into a smaller breakfast room they must use when it was only the family eating.

"I'm sorry to interrupt your meal," Juliana said, clasping her hands together.

"You seem upset. What's happened?"

"Audlington has left, and I don't know where he's gone."

Cecilia sucked in a breath. "He didn't tell you?"

"He left a very short and somewhat vague note. I wondered if someone in the household might know where he's gone. Perhaps the coachmen or grooms discussed his destination?"

And what would Juliana do if she discovered his destination? Would she follow him? What good could possibly come from that?

"Actually, never mind," Juliana said calmly, ignoring the riot of emotion inside her. She'd been a fool to let herself feel. She just wanted to shut it all away behind a locked door, then hide the key where she would never find it.

"Are you certain?" Cecilia frowned. "I'm certain we can track him down."

"It isn't necessary. He said he'd come to me to explain."

"Here? You're welcome to stay as long as you like."

"No, thank you." Juliana wanted to get on the road to Skipton as soon as possible. "I do appreciate your hospitality."

Cecilia's features remained creased with distress. "You're still getting married, aren't you?"

"I think so." But with each passing hour and day, Juliana's doubt would grow.

"Come, let's get you some breakfast." Cecilia gave her a warm smile.

Juliana appreciated the woman's kindness and friendship. "Thank you, but I think I'm going to go upstairs and pack."

"Can I send some food up?" Cecilia offered.

Though she wasn't terribly hungry, Juliana didn't want to decline. "Just a small plate. Thank you."

Cecilia embraced her briefly and pressed a kiss to her cheek. "All will be well. I could see how enamored Audlington is of you—everyone could. Your love reminds me of when I fell for Cosford."

Juliana gave her a half smile. "In what way?"

"You seemed at odds at the start of the party only to fall in love before it was concluded. Cosford and I attended a Yuletide house party with our parents years ago—the intent was to match us, but we loathed each other from a house party five years prior. We began as enemies, but ended as lovers." She lowered her voice to a bare whisper. "Literally because we were trapped in a woodcutter's cottage overnight. It was a good thing we fell in love, because we would have been forced to wed either way."

"That is most fortuitous." Juliana couldn't imagine being forced to marry someone you didn't like.

"Indeed it was." Cecilia's eyes sparkled with mirth. "I'll send up a plate."

"Thank you." Before going back upstairs to pack her things, Juliana found the butler and asked to have her coach prepared. "I'll be leaving in an hour."

"Certainly, ma'am. I'll send word to the stables at once. I'm sorry Lord Audlington had to leave so early."

Unable to resist asking for more information if

it was available, she asked, "Do you know what time that was?"

"Just after dawn. He borrowed a horse, and his coach followed shortly thereafter."

"Do you know where he went?" No, she didn't want to know that! Except she did.

"I don't, but I can ask the head groom, if you like."

So she could torture herself with that knowledge and do nothing about it? "That won't be necessary. Thank you, Vernon. You run an excellent household. My maid has been outstanding."

"I'm delighted to hear that. Thank you, ma'am."

Juliana went to her room and began to pack. She'd spend one night on the road, then she'd be back in her bed the very next night. More importantly, she'd be back on her horse the morning after that.

The idea of returning to her routine began to settle the tumult of emotions Lucas had wrought. She was eager to be free of those—and of the Runaway Viscount—for good.

CHAPTER 10

A week later, after an invigorating and wonderful ride on Clio, Juliana sipped from her favorite teacup in her favorite chair in her favorite room in her small cottage. The library was the second largest room on the ground floor, next to her receiving room, but that didn't mean it was big. No, it was compact and cozy, with shelves of books, and windows with three different views as they allowed her to look out the front, side, and back of the house.

"Afternoon, Mrs. Holloway," the deep voice of her brother-in-law, Lowther Sheldon, carried from the entrance hall.

The housekeeper tried to tell him that Juliana wasn't receiving, but it was of no use. Lowther barged into the library, his hat in his hand.

"Afternoon, Juliana," Lowther said, wiping the back of his hand over his wide, shiny forehead. His blond hair had receded several inches.

"Afternoon, Lowther," she murmured before taking another sip of tea. "I was just about to go for a walk." She wasn't, but she would gladly crawl the two miles to town if it meant he would leave.

"I won't stay long," he said as he perched on the settee near her chair.

"Lovely." Juliana wondered when he would get to his point. He always had a reason for visiting. Often, he sang the praises of his best friend, Piers Clementson, who'd been trying to court Juliana for nearly three years now.

"You've recovered from the house party by now?" Lowther asked, settling back onto the settee, indicating his visit would not be as brief as he'd stated.

"Quite." Juliana couldn't yet convince herself that she'd felt nothing more than lust for Lucas, but she was working very hard on that.

"Excellent. I've invited Piers to dinner tomorrow night, and you must join us."

Juliana gave him a bland smile. "I'm afraid I can't. I'm already dining with one of my friends." She wasn't, but she'd make plans to as soon as he left.

Lowther frowned, his thin lips practically disappearing. "The night after, then."

"That's when I play cards." *That* was true.

"You are far too busy." He let out a fake laugh that grated Juliana's ears. "Then the following night, and I shan't take no for an answer."

Before the house party, Juliana would have surrendered and forced herself to suffer through an abbreviated evening at the house—she'd beg off early due to a headache. However, after feeling like a fool a second time, she'd decided she was going to do precisely what she wanted when she wanted. And she did *not* want to dine with Lowther or his friend. Honestly, she loved everything about her place in life except her proximity to her noxious, nosy brother-in-law.

"No, Lowther," she said firmly. "I am not

coming to dinner with you and Mr. Clementson. You keep trying to make a match, and I must inform you, yet again, that I've no interest in marrying him or anyone else. You must cease your meddling, and you must stop barging into my house uninvited." She rose from the chair and stiffened her spine. "Please leave so I may take my walk."

Lowther stared up at her, his jaw working. He opened his mouth, then clamped it shut again. Finally, he stood. "There's no call to be rude."

"I'm not being rude. I'm being clear. At least, I hope I am. Do you understand that you are not to come into my house unless you are invited?"

He gaped at her.

"Answer me, please."

"Yes."

She could hear his teeth grating together. "And do you understand that I've no wish to wed Mr. Clementson, and you will cease your efforts to match us together?"

"I suppose," he muttered.

"Please say you understand, Lowther." She spoke loudly but didn't yell. It was difficult because she wanted to shout and use several unladylike words.

"I understand you don't wish to marry Piers. He will be devastated."

"I daresay he will recover." Juliana knew Piers's only interest in her was the settlement Lowther's brother had left her. She had an interest in the estate, and marriage to Piers would give it to him.

"You're making a grave mistake. Vincent would want you to be happy, and Piers would do that."

Juliana didn't bother explaining that Vincent knew leaving her a settlement so she could be independent would make her happy, not marrying someone she didn't care for. She wished she could thank him for having the forethought to ensure she was able to lead the life she wanted with the freedom to make her own choices.

"You're smiling!" Lowther crowed in an accusatory tone. "You *know* Piers would make you happy. Ha!"

"I'm going to refrain from telling you that I was imagining Vincent laughing at your proposition. The very reason he ensured I had a comfortable settlement was so that I would have the freedom to remain unwed." He'd told her that before he died, and it honestly made her wonder if he hadn't loved her at least a little, even though he'd never said so. Or perhaps Vincent had known his brother would be a colossal pain in her arse, and he'd wanted to ensure she could stand against him. Either way, she was quite grateful to her former husband in that moment.

Lowther sputtered. "Vincent would never have laughed at the suggestion you remarry."

Juliana waved him toward the door. "Time for you to go, Lowther. You did say you wouldn't stay long, and you are coming very close to...long."

Scowling, he made his way to the doorway of the library and tried to turn back toward her. However, Juliana gave him a tight smile just before she slammed the door in his face.

She heard him muttering about ungratefulness and offensive independence before the exterior door shut. Opening the library door the barest crack, she looked to see if Mrs. Holloway was in the entrance hall.

The housekeeper, who was also Juliana's lady's maid, an extremely orderly woman in her middle fifties, stood in the center of the hall, her lips pursed. She sent a nod toward Juliana before turning and retreating to the back of the house, where she would no doubt make her way down to the kitchen to assist the cook with dinner. Or, more likely, drink a cup of tea and tell the cook what had happened with Lowther. That made Juliana smile—it wasn't so much gossip as a show of support for Juliana.

A knock sounded on the exterior door. "The bloody blockhead doesn't know when to leave well enough alone," she muttered as she stamped through the entrance hall.

Juliana threw open the door, eager to give Lowther another earful. Only it wasn't her brother-in-law. And her ire didn't remotely dissipate. If anything, it burned hotter.

Crossing her arms over her chest, she glowered at the new arrival. "Well, if it isn't the Runaway Viscount."

~

The anticipation—and anxiety—rushing through Lucas ran straight into icy disdain in the form of Juliana. He knew she'd be angry, and he didn't blame her. But he supposed he'd also hoped she might be a tiny bit happy to see him.

She clearly was *not*.

"I deserve that," he said evenly. "However, I did leave you a note this time."

"The end result was the same." Her tone was cool. Dispassionate. "You left."

"For a very good reason."

"That you were inexplicably unable to detail in your note. Nor did you awaken me and explain in person."

"I had to leave immediately. The situation was

dire." Lucas's heart twisted as he recalled the desperation he'd felt when he'd received the early morning missive with absolutely unimaginable news. "I borrowed a horse from Cosford so I could leave immediately." He'd barely even dressed. His cravat had come unknotted the moment he'd put the horse into a gallop.

"I am aware of that." She exhaled. "Lucas, why are you here?"

He blinked at her. "I told you I would come. It was never my intent to leave you. We are betrothed. I love you." Was it possible she'd fallen out of love with him in a week's time?

One of her dark brows rose. "We are to pick right up where we were when you abandoned me a second time?"

Her sarcasm reminded him of her behavior when they'd encountered each other at the house party barely a fortnight ago. Perhaps she meant to torture him again.

"I will endure whatever punishment you wish to mete out, my love, but please allow me to explain. There is something I'd planned to tell you as soon as we left the party. Perhaps I should have told you sooner." He swallowed and confessed the rest—his fear. "I worried you would be upset. Or worse. That you would change your mind about me."

She uncrossed her arms as her forehead creased. "I can't think of anything that would have prompted me to change my mind. Save you running away again. Which is precisely what you did. I'm still waiting for the reason."

"It may be best if I show you." Lucas flexed and unflexed his hands as he strode back to his coach. He opened the door to see his daughter asleep on the nurse's lap. "I want to bring her inside, but I also don't want to disturb her."

"It's all right, my lord. She's been fidgeting. I suspect she's on the verge of awakening. Do you want me to bring her?"

"I'd like to take her, if that's all right."

"Of course it is," the nurse, a kindly woman in her forties, said with a warm smile. "She is your daughter."

He was still getting used to that. Knowing he had a daughter and spending time with her were different things.

The nurse transferred Alicia to Lucas. "Shall I follow you?"

"Give us a few minutes, if you please."

Nodding, the nurse remained in the coach while Lucas carried Alicia toward the cottage. At ten months, she was a solid little body in his arms, quite different from the last time he'd seen her four months ago.

He set his gaze on Juliana as he walked up the path. Her eyes widened and settled on Alicia.

When he reached the door, he spoke softly. "Juliana, this is my daughter, Alicia."

"Your daughter." Juliana stared at the child, her lips slightly parted. Then she looked at him. "I don't understand." She shook her head. "Wait. Come inside." She stepped aside for him to move into the cottage.

After she closed the door, she led him to the right into a cozy room with bookshelves and rough-hewn beams across the ceiling.

Alicia lifted her head from his shoulder. She blinked her gray eyes—his eyes—and glanced around at the new surroundings.

Lucas kissed the soft down of her light brown hair. "My darling." He looked over at Juliana. "Her mother was my mistress during the Season after we met at the Pack Horse. I took her on, hoping to banish you from my mind. It didn't work. I ended the arrangement after a month. Another instance of my running away, I suppose. However, that was all it took for her to get with child."

"With Alicia?" Juliana couldn't seem to look away from his daughter.

He couldn't tell what she was thinking. "Yes."

"Come and sit." Juliana led him to a settee and sat down. "How old is she?"

Lucas lowered himself and Alicia to the cushion, cradling her against his shoulder as she slowly roused from sleep. "Ten months. She and her mother were living in Manchester. I supported them entirely, and I was to visit twice yearly." At that moment, Juliana's gaze flicked to Lucas. "I should have told you about them, about the situation, when I proposed."

"Why didn't you?"

He tried to find the words. "I don't really know. I suppose I was overcome with what was happening between us. Or perhaps it was me avoiding something difficult yet again. I've done that a great deal in my life, which I didn't realize until you."

"What do you mean?"

"You calling me the Runaway Viscount was rather apt. I think I was running away from anything that pushed me toward responsibility and ultimately love. Our conversations at the Pack Horse are what prompted me to stand for Parliament. And I believe you're the reason I allowed myself to love Alicia. Our time together two years ago may have been short, but I think you opened my heart. When we were reunited at Blickton, it was the first time I wanted to run *to* something—or someone. Even knowing you couldn't have children and after the pain of not raising Alicia, I wanted to be with you. Life is messy and unexpected and...*real*. Instead of running from it, I want to embrace every moment with you by my side."

All while he'd talked, Juliana had watched him intently, her eyes taking on a sheen of unshed tears by the time he finished. "I've struggled with the same thing," she said softly. "I may not have run away exactly, but I've avoided allowing myself to feel. But I told you that when I decided to accept your marriage proposal. I confess I'm still finding it hard to do that, especially after you left me again, even though I know you had a very good reason for it." She looked toward Alicia.

"I'm so damned sorry I didn't tell you before." If he lost her, he wasn't sure he'd ever recover. Because it would be entirely his fault. "I'd planned to tell you when we departed Blickton. But something awful happened."

Juliana paled. "Where is her mother? I notice you are speaking about the situation with her in the past tense."

"There was an accident. They were riding in a coach, and something malfunctioned. It veered off the road into a tree. Caroline—her mother—died."

A soft gasp burst from Juliana, and Alicia startled. "I'm sorry, sweetling," Juliana said before glancing back at Lucas. "The baby was fine? What a miracle."

Alicia began to fidget, and Lucas turned her so she could sit on his lap while he kept his arm around her waist. He reached into his coat pocket and withdrew a thick, smooth piece of coral for her to chew on.

"This is for her as she has teeth breaking through." Lucas put the coral into Alicia's hand, and it went immediately into her mouth. "Yes, it was a miracle," he murmured, responding to Juliana. "As soon as I received word of the accident, I rushed to Manchester. I should have awakened you, but I was too distraught. I could think of nothing but my daughter."

"As you should have done," Juliana whispered. "I don't blame you. I would have done the same." She shook her head. "How have you managed?"

Lucas felt an immense relief that she understood. "It's been a challenge, I admit. I spent several days in Manchester arranging for Caroline's burial and closing up the house, as well as finding a nurse who was willing to travel with us."

"No, I mean how did you manage being apart from your daughter. I can see how deeply you care for her."

"Can you? We've only just arrived."

Juliana smiled at him. "I've come to know you rather well. You hold her with a possessiveness and love that only a father would do with his child."

"You don't think me awful for fathering an illegitimate child?"

"How could I when you've gone to every effort to provide for her—and her mother? Are you going to raise her now?"

This was where the anxiety lived. Lucas was going to ask a great deal of this woman he loved. "I was hoping we would raise her together, that we might adopt her and give her my name. But I realize that not everyone would want to raise another—"

"Stop." Juliana held out her arms. "May I?"

"Of course." Lucas gave Alicia into Juliana's care.

"What a beautiful girl you are," Juliana said softly, her smile bright. "What are you chewing on there? Does that feel good for your teeth?"

"The nurse says the coral helps."

"You found a nurse, then?" Juliana asked. "Where is she?"

"In the coach. I said we needed a few minutes."

"You must fetch her. I'm sure she'll want to stretch her legs." Juliana stroked Alicia's hair. "Unless… Are you going to stay?"

"I'd hoped to." Lucas honestly hadn't known what to expect. But perhaps he should have. Didn't he know Juliana well enough to realize she wouldn't have shrunk from this? Or was he worried she didn't love him as much as he loved her?

"Do you want us to stay?" he asked. "I know it's a great deal to ask, expecting you to be an instant mother."

"I think I've wanted to be a mother for nearly a decade," Juliana said, smiling again. "I didn't expect I would ever have the chance."

He hadn't realized that, but then she hadn't really shared the sentiment with him. She'd said she couldn't be a mother, never that she'd wanted to be. He recalled her fear about their marriage failing as hers with Vincent had done. Perhaps she feared telling him that she'd wanted children. If that were the case, it was likely that she was even more worried about him resenting her in the future if they weren't able to have any.

He scooted closer to her. "If we do not have any children of our own, I would be more than eager to find others to adopt."

Juliana let out a laugh that sounded suspiciously like a sob. She briefly clapped her hand over her mouth. "How many others?" Her eyes glimmered with happiness.

"As many as you like."

"You won't care if they aren't of your blood?"

Lucas watched her hold his daughter—their

daughter. "I can see that it doesn't matter to you that Alicia isn't yours."

"Not my blood, no," Juliana said softly. She bent her head and gently kissed Alicia's crown. "But I will be your mother, and it will be my great privilege."

"I didn't think it was possible that I could love you more." There was a near pain in his chest, his joy was so great.

She looked up at him, her head still against Alicia's. "This is real, then? We love each other, and we're to be a family?"

"That's what I want."

"That's what I want too. Just promise you'll never leave me again." She lifted her head. "You could have come to my room and dragged me from bed. I would have accompanied you to Manchester in my nightclothes. I could have helped you. We are partners now. We do things together. *Promise me.*"

He wished he'd awakened her too. She would have made the last week more bearable. He hadn't loved Caroline, but he'd been terribly sad for Alicia that her mother had died. It wasn't fair. And yet, Alicia would grow up in a family with love and care. "I promise. Together."

"Good." Juliana adopted a businesslike tone that he thoroughly expected and adored. "Now, go fetch the nurse, and we'll set up the guest room for her and Alicia. I've no cradle, but surely we can find something."

"I have one on the back of the coach."

"Excellent. How long do you wish to stay before we go to Leeds to visit my parents?" Juliana shook her head. "Never mind that now. We'll decide later. We have plenty of time."

Yes, they had a lifetime. Except Lucas was eager

for them to be wed. "Not too much time, if you don't mind. I'm keen to make you my wife. If you are still amenable."

"Of course I am." She laughed. "Don't be daft. Yes, we will wed as soon as possible. I'm sure we can go to Leeds tomorrow, if you think Alicia is ready to travel again so soon."

"The nurse says it's no problem. I feel rather worthless. I don't know the first thing about being a parent."

"I don't either, but I daresay we'll find out quickly."

"Together," he said.

She dropped another kiss on Alicia's head. "Together."

CHAPTER 11

*J*uliana looked over at Lucas, who was holding their daughter, as they walked to the massive oak door of Northwich Hall. The visit with her parents had gone exceedingly well, and they would arrive here in a fortnight to celebrate and attend the wedding. The planning of that had felt somewhat strange since Lucas's parents were, as yet, completely unaware that their son was betrothed.

Or that he had a child.

He hadn't wanted to tell them in writing, insisting that it would be better to deliver this news in person. She'd questioned him, but ultimately decided he was right. Juliana would not have wanted to learn about Alicia in a note. Even if it meant he'd kept her waiting a week and made it look, unintentionally, as if he'd abandoned her again.

The door opened, and a squat, austere-faced butler greeted them. "Welcome home, my lord." He didn't reflect the slightest reaction to Lucas carrying a child, to the unknown woman beside him, or to the other woman who stood behind them—Alicia's nurse. The butler did glance in Juliana's di-

rection, but that was the extent of his acknowledgment.

"Good to see you, Graham. Are my parents in
the drawing room?" Lucas had sent word ahead
last night that he would be arriving today.

"The library, actually."

"Thank you." Lucas turned slight toward Juliana, his free hand grazing her lower back. "May I
present Mrs. Sheldon. That is all I shall say on the
matter at the moment. Please refrain from allowing anyone to discuss her arrival or that of the
child I'm carrying. Or the child's nurse." He
glanced back at Mrs. Talmidge. "All will be revealed after I have spoken with the earl and
countess."

Graham sniffed. "I would never allow gossip in
the servants' hall."

Lucas gave him a warm smile. "Of course not.
Still, sometimes it's wise to say such things out
loud, just to be sure."

Juliana wondered if other servants might be listening. She glanced around the wide, elegant entrance hall and noted a footman standing on the
opposite side. His features and posture were as im-
placable as the butler's.

Graham inclined his head, and Lucas murmured to Juliana that the library was in the right
corner at the back of the ground floor. He guided
her through the staircase hall, gleaming with dark
wood and featuring a great many paintings. It was,
in a word, overwhelming to think she would live
here, at least sometimes. And someday, it would be
her household. Doubt stole over her. Could she really be a countess?

They passed through a few rooms, each more
beautiful than the last. It was one thing to visit a

house like this, such as Blickton for a party, but to live here?

At last, they entered a small sitting room. Lucas gestured to a doorway. "There's the library. Ready?"

"As I will ever be, I suppose," Juliana said, a tense anxiety swirling through her. She looked to Alicia, who was furiously chewing on her coral. One of her bottom teeth had broken through while they were visiting Juliana's parents. Her mother had been incredibly helpful sharing her own experience rearing children. She'd shown Juliana how to make a poultice that would ease the pain of the tooth erupting. They rubbed it on Alicia's gums, particularly at night before bed, and it worked very well to soothe the child.

Lucas turned to Mrs. Talmidge. "Would you mind waiting here while we go in to speak with my parents? I'll call for you if we require assistance with Alicia."

Mrs. Talmidge nodded. "Of course, my lord." She went to sit in a chair near the door leading to the library.

"Come, my darling," Lucas said to Alicia. "Time to meet your grandparents."

Alicia let out a happy, gurgling sound. She liked to babble on occasion, and Juliana's mother had said that her first words would likely come soon.

They walked into the library. Orderly bookshelves bearing leather-bound books stretched along one wall, and there were three seating areas, including several cozy chairs near the fire. For the first time, Juliana could envision herself living there—that area was most inviting.

"Audlington." The earl rose from a settee in the seating arrangement closest to where they entered. The countess remained seated.

Lucas's father looked rather like him, though he was a couple of inches shorter. His hair was mostly gray, but there were a few bits of brown here and there. His blue eyes fixed on Alicia.

"Father," Lucas said. "Mother."

"You are not alone," the countess said. Her gray gaze—which was very much like Lucas's—moved between Alicia and Juliana.

"I am not." Lucas turned to Juliana. "Allow me to present my betrothed, Mrs. Juliana Sheldon. We met at Blickton at a house party recently."

The countess leapt up from the settee. "And she has a child into the bargain?"

"Er, no." Lucas took a deep breath. "Mama, Father, this is *my* daughter, Alicia."

"*Your* daughter?" the earl's deep voice had risen slightly, and his nostrils flared.

Tensing, Juliana moved closer to Lucas so that their arms touched.

"Yes." Lucas spoke clearly and evenly. "Her mother was my mistress, and I'm sorry to say that she died recently. Juliana and I will raise the child as our own."

The earl gaped at his son. "You can't be serious. She's illegitimate! How can you even be sure she's yours?"

"Because I am," Lucas said firmly. Juliana could practically hear his jaw clenching. She certainly felt the anguish stiffening his frame. Alicia felt it too, for she began to fuss.

"Let me," Juliana murmured, taking the baby from him. Alicia eagerly grabbed at Juliana with the hand that wasn't clutching the coral.

The countess came toward Juliana, her gaze fixed on Alicia. "She is our granddaughter. You've only to look at her eyes." She smiled warmly. "How lovely you are, my dear."

"She truly is," Juliana said, stroking Alicia's head.

"How old is she?" the countess asked.

"Just over ten months," Juliana responded.

"And she's getting teeth, I see. Is she crawling around yet?"

Juliana smiled. "She is trying to." Alicia had begun scooting on her belly while they'd visited Juliana's parents.

"That's it, then?" the earl asked, sounding irritated. "We're just to accept our son's illegitimate daughter?" He speared his son with a glower of stark disappointment. "I warned you that your behavior would embarrass the family. You promised me it wouldn't."

"And it won't. I am marrying Juliana, and we will raise Alicia as our child."

"People will talk and speculate!" The earl turned and stalked away.

"Let him be for a moment," the countess said softly. She looked to Juliana. "I am pleased to meet you. The woman who has finally captured Lucas's heart must be very special indeed."

Juliana felt a burst of warmth for this woman and sensed they would get on very well, just as Lucas had assured her. "Thank you. I love him very much."

"And yes, Mama, she has captured my heart completely. As has Alicia."

"I can see why. She is precious." The countess looked to Lucas. "I can't imagine this has been easy. You possess such a sensitive nature. I now understand why your behavior changed so abruptly over the past year."

"You noticed that?" Lucas had explained to Juliana how he'd stopped taking lovers after Caroline and that he'd just about become a monk until he'd encountered her at Blickton.

"Mothers notice everything, dear." She sent a smile toward Juliana, her gray eyes twinkling. "You'll find out."

That the countess recognized Juliana as a mother made her throat ache. She'd never imagined to have that title, and to her it was far better than that of viscountess or countess.

"I suppose Father didn't notice," Lucas said, his gaze moving toward the windows on the far side of the room, where the earl was now standing, his back to them.

"He did once I drew his attention to it," the countess said. "Just as I will draw his attention to how this is a joyful occasion and a wonderful beginning for you and your new family. In the meantime, let us discuss some specifics. Juliana—is it all right that I call you that?"

"Of course."

"Good, and you may call me Peggy. Please sit beside me so I can dote on my granddaughter." She sat back down on the settee, and Juliana went to where the earl had been sitting when they'd entered.

Lucas took a chair near the settee, his features a mix of happiness as he smiled at his mother and concern as he kept flicking glances toward his father. "We would like to wed in the church with the banns read this Sunday."

"Wonderful," Peggy said. "The vicar will be so pleased. And your brother and his family will be here next week, so we'll all be together."

"Will we?" Lucas asked, once again shooting a glance at his father.

"Yes," his mother responded firmly. "Your father will come around. Quickly, I will add." She gave the earl a look that all but commanded his capitulation.

Juliana heard the confidence and slight edge of annoyance in Peggy's tone and decided she was a formidable woman. Hopefully, the next part of the conversation would go smoothly. "We'd like to discuss lodging arrangements. We don't expect to reside together, of course, but Lucas and I would both like to sleep in the same building as Alicia and her nurse."

"I'm so glad you have a nurse," Peggy said. "Where is she?"

Lucas gestured toward the door through which they'd entered. "Mrs. Talmidge is in the sitting room. She is, unfortunately, not permanent, as she would like to return to Manchester where her children live."

"I see. Well, we will hire a nurse as soon as possible." Peggy looked to Alicia. "I promise we will find someone who will love you as we do."

Alicia fixed her wide-eyed gaze on Peggy and babbled.

Peggy smiled at her. "I am your grandmama. We will get to know each other very well." She looked to Lucas. "You'll be staying through Epiphany at least?"

He nodded. "We'll stay until I need to return to London."

"Wonderful. You can have the northeast wing, of course."

"That's where my chamber is located," Lucas said to Juliana.

"There's an entire suite of rooms that will accommodate all of you," Peggy said. "We'll trust you to comport yourselves with propriety until the wedding."

"You can't think Audlington can be trusted?"

The earl had apparently walked back toward them and now stood in the middle of the library, his features drawn into deep lines.

"Of course he can." Peggy narrowed her eyes at her husband. "He has never brought disgrace to this family, and he never will. Come and meet your soon-to-be daughter-in-law and your granddaughter. Be angry with Lucas if you must, but don't extend that emotion to them—not unless you want their first impression of you to be a rather poor one."

Juliana hadn't yet formed a solid opinion of the earl. Lucas had prepared her for his disdain, but also assured her that he would put it behind him. The question was how quickly that would happen.

The earl grunted a response, then came over to where they were sitting. He looked at Alicia, his mouth set into a slight frown. "I suppose she does have your eyes," he said to his wife.

"And Lucas's," Peggy said.

The earl turned his attention to Juliana. "I will hope that you have tamed my son. He certainly needed it."

Had Lucas really been that wild? She didn't think he'd done anything terrible, and his mother seemed to confirm this. Juliana would ask him later. "Your son is a wonderful man and father. I will hope that these aspects will never be tamed out of him."

Peggy laughed softly. "Spoken like a loving, protective wife. Well done, my dear."

The earl scowled. Then he directed a glare at his son. "Audlington, my study. Now." The earl stalked from the room, using a doorway situated in the row of bookshelves.

"I should probably go," Lucas said to Juliana.

Juliana transferred Alicia to the other side of her lap. "Go on, we'll be fine."

Peggy gave him a steady look as he rose. "Don't tolerate any of his nonsense."

"I try not to, Mama." Lucas moved around the settee and bussed his mother's cheek before departing the library.

"Now, let me ring for some refreshments," Peggy said, standing. "And do invite the nurse in."

"Thank you, Peggy. For everything." It was the warmest welcome Juliana could have hoped for. She only hoped things between Lucas and his father improved sooner rather than later.

~

*L*ucas closed the door to the study after he stepped over the threshold. "Could you not have been more polite to Juliana? She doesn't deserve your derision."

His father stood near the hearth, a deep scowl etched into his features. "I was perfectly polite to her. I didn't hide my disappointment in *you*. If she wishes to be your wife, she can't wilt from family."

"Juliana won't wilt from anything," Lucas said with a slight smile. "You'll learn that soon enough."

"I can gather that since she's willing to raise your child."

"Not just willing, but eager." Lucas saw no point in avoiding the inevitable conversation. "I know you think less of me for having her."

"I cautioned you against fathering children. There are ways to avoid such…problems."

Lucas couldn't think of his daughter as a problem, even as he knew what his father meant. More than that, he'd thought of children in much the same way in his younger years. He'd done his part to try to avoid the creation of a child, but nothing was infallible. "You know it can't always be prevented." Lucas exhaled, hoping his father could get past his anger. "Father, I am not going to debate the existence of my daughter. I love Alicia, and I am honored and thrilled to raise her. It broke my heart to leave her after she was born."

His father snapped his gaze to Lucas's. "You've been involved with this child all along?"

"Yes. I made sure her mother and she were cared for—and that they always would be. When her mother died a fortnight ago, I rushed to fetch Alicia."

"For years, I've tried to see you wed with children, to take on some responsibility beyond visiting our other properties. I was encouraged when you stood for Parliament, and I expected you would finally wed this coming Season."

"Because you said I must," Lucas reminded him.

"But this is what provoked you finally—an illegitimate child?"

"Actually, no. Well, perhaps in part. But what inspired me to stand for Parliament was meeting Juliana nearly two years ago." Lucas took a step toward his father. "She affected me in ways I couldn't have imagined. Before her, I just felt aimless, and yes, I avoided responsibility. More importantly, I avoided anything that would result in permanence or expectation. I also didn't want to fail at love— not with you and Mother as an example."

His father was quiet a moment, his brow creasing. "I didn't realize you felt that way, that you were…"

"Cowardly? Afraid?" Lucas let out a short self-deprecating laugh.

"No, not that. Vulnerable, perhaps. I do love your mother most fiercely, and I know our marriage is different from many in our class. I can imagine you felt pressure to find something like we have—and it isn't easy."

"It absolutely is not. After Jonathan and Hetty fell in love, I was certain it couldn't happen for me. No family is that lucky to have so much love."

The earl's features softened in a way Lucas had never witnessed. "Apparently, ours is. You love Mrs. Sheldon as much as I love your mother and as much as your brother loves his wife. It's good that you waited. Clearly, you were meant to."

"Thank you, Father." Love made Lucas's heart swell. "She is everything I ever could have hoped for."

Moving toward Lucas, his father pressed his lips into a grim line. "You know there will be talk about your daughter."

"I plan to ignore it."

"Good, but it will still be there, and questions will follow her. You need to be prepared for that."

Lucas wasn't going to run away from his daughter—not now and not ever. "She will always have my full support and my unconditional love. I hope you will give her the same."

The earl's face relaxed once more, and this time, he even smiled. "Seeing you happy is all I've ever wanted. You're a parent now, so you'll find that out for yourself."

Lucas already knew. There was nothing he wouldn't do for Alicia. "I am happier than I ever hoped I could be, thanks to Juliana."

"Then I suppose I should go back and apologize to her. I look forward to knowing her."

"And loving her," Lucas said with a smile. "You won't be able to resist."

CHAPTER 12

*J*uliana stood in the small sitting room in the vicar's house next to the church in Northwich as her mother made her final perusal of her gown. The ceremony was due to start in a few minutes.

"You look lovely," her mother said, her blue-green eyes bright. "Is it just me, or does this time seem different?"

"In what way?" Juliana asked, though it was an absurd question. Marrying Lucas was different from marrying Vincent in just about every way. But Juliana wanted to hear her mother's perspective. She and her father had arrived a few days ago, and they'd got on very well with Lucas's parents. Juliana hadn't been worried. She'd come to know Peggy and Northwich and had no concern they would treat her parents with anything but respect and kindness. Indeed, they'd ended up having many interests in common, such as cards, and their fathers had read many of the same books. The earl was delighted to have a bookseller in the family.

"It's obvious that Audlington loves you," Juliana's sister answered. Two years older than Juliana, Ellen typically said precisely what she was thinking. "Vincent cared for you, but I didn't see the deeper emotion Audlington displays. It's lovely." Ellen gave her sister a wide grin.

"I would agree with that assessment," their mother said. She took Juliana's hand and gave her a squeeze. "I'm so very happy for you, my darling."

"Thank you, Mama." Juliana had never imagined doing this a second time, but in some ways, it felt as though she'd never done it at all. Her mother and sister were right that this—Lucas—was completely different.

The door opened, and Juliana immediately tensed. It was likely the vicar's wife informing them it was time. A kindly woman in her sixties, Mrs. Linley gave them a somewhat nervous smile. Juliana's tension shifted into something more like concern.

"The ceremony is going to be slightly delayed," she said.

Ellen moved toward Mrs. Linley from the window where she'd been standing. "What is the problem?"

Mrs. Linley glanced toward Juliana before looking at their mother of all people. "We're waiting on his lordship. The groom, that is. He has not yet arrived."

Juliana's heart beat faster. He wouldn't abandon her again. There was nothing that would keep him from their wedding. She had no doubts about that at all. What was going on, then?

"Do you know why?" Juliana asked.

The vicar's wife shook her head. "I do not."

"It's fine. Thank you, Mrs. Linley. Do let us know when the viscount arrives."

After Mrs. Linley left, Juliana went to the window and looked toward the church.

"Are you watching for him?" her mother asked.

She supposed she was, and that would only ex-acerbate her anxiety. But why was she anxious? She'd already determined she wasn't concerned, that she trusted he would be there.

Her mind turned to possible reasons for him being late. There was only one thing that would prevent him from being here on time. Rather, one person.

Juliana turned from the window. "His delay must be something to do with Alicia. I should re-turn to Northwich Hall."

Her mother's brow creased. "You'll wrinkle your dress if you get in a coach. If Alicia is the is-sue, Lucas can handle things. He's an excellent father."

That was certainly true. Watching him with his daughter never failed to make Juliana smile and her heart swell to two times its size. Seeing them together, she was so glad for Alicia, especially since she doubted they'd have children of their own.

"You're right," Juliana said. "We must simply wait, then."

After a quarter hour of moving about the room, Juliana was beginning to grow frustrated. It wasn't even that Lucas was still missing—though that was certainly part of it—but that she couldn't sit in her gown.

Ellen had positioned herself at the window so she could watch. Finally, she turned. "He's coming. Running, actually."

Juliana hurried to the window to see Lucas tearing toward the vicarage. She made her way to the door.

"Stop, you can't go meet him," her mother cried. "It's bad luck."

"I don't believe in that nonsense." Juliana had avoided seeing Vincent and look how their marriage had turned out. She opened the door and heard Mrs. Linley speaking to Lucas.

"I just need to see her for a moment," he was saying from the small entry hall. "Alicia was terribly fussy, and I couldn't leave her."

Juliana smiled. Of course it had been Alicia.

"I can't let you see her," Mrs. Linley said firmly. "It's bad luck."

"What's bad luck is my bride thinking I am not coming to our wedding."

Juliana heard the anxiety in his voice. "Lucas, I hear you. I wasn't worried." She stepped into the entry hall, and Lucas's gaze met hers. The lines in his face smoothed, and a broad smile split his face.

"You look beautiful," he whispered.

Mrs. Linley gasped. "Oh dear, this is a calamity."

"It isn't, truly," Juliana assured her. "There will be no bad luck. Will you give us a moment alone?" she asked the woman.

After sputtering a moment, Mrs. Linley reluctantly nodded. "Just a moment." Her brow furrowed in distress, she departed the entry hall, leaving them alone.

"Are you terribly angry with me?" Lucas asked.

"Not at all. I said I wasn't worried, and I meant it."

"My record of abandonment didn't concern you at all?"

"I'd be lying if I said it didn't cross my mind, but I am quite confident in our love for one another. You wouldn't abandon me today of all days. I determined there had to be a problem with Alicia. I heard what you said. Is she all right?"

"Mostly. She's still fussing, but I brought her to the church to sit with Grandmama. She was preferable to the new nurse—I'm afraid Alicia still hasn't grown used to her yet." Their plan had been for Alicia not to attend the ceremony. She would stay with her nurse and attend a portion of the wedding breakfast gathering.

"So she'll be at the wedding, then?" Juliana asked.

"You don't mind?"

"Not at all. In fact, I'm rather pleased by it," she admitted.

"Even if she's disruptive? She may cry. I think she has an upset belly."

"That you are aware of our daughter's ills makes me so very happy. I could not have imagined a more perfect husband and father." Juliana threw her arms around him and embraced him tightly.

He held her close and brushed his lips against her temple. "Thank you. That's perhaps the nicest thing anyone has ever said to me."

Juliana pulled back. "And no, I don't care if our daughter cries during our wedding ceremony. Do you?"

He shook his head. "I only care that you love me."

"Then it's a good thing that I do. With all my heart."

Lucas caressed her cheek, his eyes shining with love. "I am the luckiest man alive."

"You won't be if you don't get to the church," Juliana said, glancing behind her toward where Mrs. Linley was likely lurking. "Go. I'll see you shortly."

"That you will, my love. And then you will be mine forevermore."

EPILOGUE

Epiphany 1807

"*M*ama!"

Juliana turned to her daughter, who was excitedly clapping her hands. "What is it, dearest?"

"Look at Christopher!" She pointed to her younger brother, who was walking toward them.

Gasping, Juliana dropped the toys she'd been picking up. "Lucas, come here!"

He was right next door in his study and rushed in barely a moment later. His gaze settled on his son, whose forehead was puckered in deep concentration as he made his way toward Juliana.

"He's walking," Lucas breathed. They'd worried when he'd taken so much longer to ambulate than Alicia. She'd started just after turning a year old, while Christopher was now sixteen months. He was an expert crawler and used the furniture to stand and move. But today, he was walking by himself—and Alicia had been the first to witness it.

"It's a miracle, Papa," Alicia said. At four, she

was precocious and talkative. Her favorite thing was managing her little brother.

"It is indeed, my sweet." Lucas met Juliana's gaze, and she knew he was referring to Christopher himself, not that he was walking.

When Juliana had become pregnant, she hadn't really believed it. She hadn't told a soul until it became obvious to Lucas. He'd noticed her belly curving, and she'd promptly burst into tears as she'd revealed the truth.

Now they had Christopher, a son they never expected and wholly adored.

"That's the way, my boy." Lucas sat on the floor, encouraging Christopher.

Juliana went down beside him and resisted the urge to hold out her hands to Christopher as he wobbled. If he fell, as he had so many times in his efforts, he didn't have far to go. And he always landed on his rump with the exclamation, "Oh dear," which he'd gleaned from hearing Juliana say it.

Christopher at last reached them, and Lucas pulled him onto his lap. "You did it!"

Squirming, Christopher said, "Go!"

Lucas released him with a chuckle, setting him on his feet. "Yes, go. Walk to your sister now."

Alicia stood on the other side of the room. "Come, Christopher. I will give you a biscuit." She looked to Juliana. "He surely deserves a biscuit?"

"I think so," Juliana said.

They watched Christopher make his way back across the room, displaying a bit more confidence, if not speed. When he reached Alicia, she put her arms around him and patted his back. "Well done, Christopher."

He hugged her back, and Juliana felt tears clog her throat. To think that a few short years ago she had none of this, nor any expectation for it. Her life was wonderfully, impossibly full.

She turned her head toward her husband. "Thank you," she whispered.

Alarm flickered in his gaze, but then he smiled. He lifted his hand to caress her cheek. "Don't cry, my love."

"They would be happy tears."

"Then cry away." He leaned over and kissed her cheek. "I know what you're thinking," he said softly. "And I'm thinking it too. Seeing each other before our wedding was the opposite of bad luck."

"My good fortune started the day I was stranded at an inn during a snowstorm."

"And took a respite when I abandoned you there." Lucas grimaced. "I still can't believe you decided to welcome me back into your life."

"You earned it after a great deal of torment. That was rather delightful, I must admit."

He laughed. "Termagant."

"You loved every moment," Juliana said, rolling her eyes.

"I did indeed." His eyes sparked with heat. "Promise to torture me later?"

"Always."

Don't miss THE MAKE-BELIEVE WIDOW, the next enchanting book in the Matchmaking Chronicles! Find out what happens when the Earl of Rotherham decides widow Charlotte Dunthorpe will be the perfect mother to his daughters. Except Charlotte is not who she claims to be....

Would you like to know when my next book is

available and to hear about sales and deals? **Sign up for my VIP newsletter** which is the only place you can get bonus books and material such as the short prequel to the Phoenix Club series, INVITATION, and the exciting prequel to Legendary Rogues, THE LEGEND OF A ROGUE.

Join me on social media!

Facebook: https://facebook.com/DarcyBurkeFans
Twitter at @darcyburke
Instagram at darcyburkeauthor
Pinterest at darcyburkewrite

And follow me on Bookbub to receive updates on pre-orders, new releases, and deals!

Need more Regency romance? Check out my other historical series:

The Phoenix Club
Society's most exclusive invitation...

Welcome to the Phoenix Club, where London's most audacious, disreputable, and intriguing ladies and gentlemen find scandal, redemption, and second chances.

The Untouchables
Swoon over twelve of Society's most eligible and elusive bachelor peers and the bluestockings, wallflowers, and outcasts who bring them to their knees!

The Untouchables: The Spitfire Society
Meet the smart, independent women who've decided they don't need Society's rules, their

families' expectations, or, most importantly, a husband. But just because they don't need a man doesn't mean they might not *want* one…

The Untouchables: The Pretenders
Set in the captivating world of The Untouchables, follow the saga of a trio of siblings who excel at being something they're not. Can a dauntless Bow Street Runner, a devastated viscount, and a disillusioned Society miss unravel their secrets?

Wicked Dukes Club
Six books written by me and my BFF, NYT Bestselling Author Erica Ridley. Meet the unforgettable men of London's most notorious tavern, The Wicked Duke. Seductively handsome, with charm and wit to spare, one night with these rakes and rogues will never be enough…

Love is All Around
Heartwarming Regency-set retellings of classic Christmas stories (written after the Regency!) featuring a cozy village, three siblings, and the best gift of all: love.

Secrets and Scandals
Six epic stories set in London's glittering ballrooms and England's lush countryside.

Legendary Rogues
Five intrepid heroines and adventurous heroes embark on exciting quests across the Georgian Highlands and Regency England and Wales!

If you like contemporary romance, I hope you'll check out my **Ribbon Ridge** series available from

Avon Impulse, and the continuation of Ribbon Ridge in **So Hot**.

I hope you'll consider leaving a review at your favorite online vendor or networking site!

I appreciate my readers so much. Thank you, thank you, *thank you.*

ALSO BY DARCY BURKE

Historical Romance

The Phoenix Club

Improper

Impassioned

Intolerable

Indecent

Impossible

Irresistible

Impeccable

Insatiable

The Matchmaking Chronicles

The Rigid Duke

The Bachelor Earl (also prequel to *The Untouchables*)

The Runaway Viscount

The Make-Believe Widow

The Unexpected Rogue

The Never Duchess

The Untouchables

The Bachelor Earl (prequel)

The Forbidden Duke

The Duke of Daring

The Duke of Deception

The Duke of Desire

The Duke of Defiance

The Duke of Danger

The Duke of Ice
The Duke of Ruin
The Duke of Lies
The Duke of Seduction
The Duke of Kisses
The Duke of Distraction

The Untouchables: The Spitfire Society

Never Have I Ever with a Duke
A Duke is Never Enough
A Duke Will Never Do

The Untouchables: The Pretenders

A Secret Surrender
A Scandalous Bargain
A Rogue to Ruin

Love is All Around

(A Regency Holiday Trilogy)
The Red Hot Earl
The Gift of the Marquess
Joy to the Duke

Wicked Dukes Club

One Night for Seduction by Erica Ridley
One Night of Surrender by Darcy Burke
One Night of Passion by Erica Ridley
One Night of Scandal by Darcy Burke
One Night to Remember by Erica Ridley
One Night of Temptation by Darcy Burke

Secrets and Scandals

Her Wicked Ways

His Wicked Heart
To Seduce a Scoundrel
To Love a Thief (a novella)
Never Love a Scoundrel
Scoundrel Ever After

Legendary Rogues
Lady of Desire
Romancing the Earl
Lord of Fortune
Captivating the Scoundrel

Contemporary Romance

Ribbon Ridge
Where the Heart Is (a prequel novella)
Only in My Dreams
Yours to Hold
When Love Happens
The Idea of You
When We Kiss
You're Still the One

Ribbon Ridge: So Hot
So Good
So Right
So Wrong

ABOUT THE AUTHOR

Darcy Burke is the USA Today Bestselling Author of sexy, emotional historical and contemporary romance. Darcy wrote her first book at age 11, a happily ever after about a swan addicted to magic and the female swan who loved him, with exceedingly poor illustrations. Join her Reader Club newsletter for the latest updates from Darcy.

A native Oregonian, Darcy lives on the edge of wine country with her guitar-strumming husband, incredibly talented artist daughter, and imaginative son who will almost certainly out-write her one day (that may be tomorrow). They're a crazy cat family with two Bengal cats, a small, fame-seeking cat named after a fruit, an older rescue Maine Coon with attitude to spare, an adorable former stray who wandered onto their deck and into their hearts, and two bonded boys who used to belong to (separate) neighbors but chose them instead. You can find Darcy at a winery, in her comfy writing chair, folding laundry (which she loves), or binge-watching TV with the family. Her happy places are Disneyland, Labor Day weekend at the Gorge, Denmark, and anywhere in the UK—so long as her family is there too. Visit Darcy online at www.darcyburke.com and follow her on social media.

facebook.com/DarcyBurkeFans

twitter.com/darcyburke

instagram.com/darcyburkeauthor

pinterest.com/darcyburkewrites

goodreads.com/darcyburke

bookbub.com/authors/darcy-burke

amazon.com/author/darcyburke

Lightning Source UK Ltd.
Milton Keynes UK
UKHW012024231222
414414UK00007B/65